stranger in dadland

Other Novels by Amy Goldman Koss

The Girls

The Ashwater Experiment

How I Saved Hanukkah

The Trouble With Zinny Weston

stranger in dadland

Amy
Goldman
Koss

Dial Books
New  York

Published by Dial Books

A division of Penguin Putnam Inc.

345 Hudson Street

New York, New York 10014

Copyright © 2001 by Amy Goldman Koss

All rights reserved

Designed by Lily Malcom

Text set in Slimbach

Printed in the U.S.A. on acid-free paper

10 9 8 7 6 5 4 3 2 1

Library of Congress Cataloging-in-Publication Data

Koss, Amy Goldman, date.

Stranger in Dadland / Amy Goldman Koss.

p. cm.

Summary: Twelve-year-old John develops a new understanding
of his divorced father during an eventful summer visit to California.

ISBN 0-8037-2563-9 (hardcover)

[1. Fathers and sons—Fiction. 2. Divorce—Fiction. 3. Interpersonal
relations—Fiction. 4. California—Fiction.]

I. Title: Stranger in Dad Land. II. Title

PZ7.K8527 St 2001

[Fic]—dc21   99-462100

Special thanks to Max Goldman,
Barry Goldman, and Peter Williamson.

This book is for you, Benny.

chapter one

The flight attendant knelt in the aisle next to me. "Anything you need, honey, just push this," she said, tapping the button *clearly* marked for calling the flight attendant. "The boys' room is down there," she added, loud enough for everyone to hear.

I wanted to snap, "I'm twelve, not three!" But instead, I grabbed a magazine out of the seat pocket and flipped it open to a picture of golf clubs. It's hard to appear suddenly fascinated by golf clubs.

Finally, we backed away from the gate, started moving faster, and lifted off. All of Kansas shrank to dots and dashes before being swallowed by clouds.

I knew my mom had waited to watch me take off. In case—what? Hostile Martians tried to hijack the plane and only Mom could reason with them? Now my sister, Liz, was probably dragging her to the parking lot, which would remind my mom that it was even more dangerous on the freeway than in the air, so she'd switch worries. Mom was a champion worrier. That was one of the reasons I was glad to be leaving: Worrying is contagious, and I didn't want to catch any more than I had already.

The man next to me opened his laptop and began typing. His fatness spilled over the armrest between us as if he were inflating. At least he was a man, so we didn't have to talk. If he'd been a woman, he probably would've asked me a million questions, would have been too friendly, babying me like the flight attendant had. Speak of the devil, she was back again, asking if I was okay.

"I fly to California for a week every summer," I muttered. "My dad lives there."

"Oh. You're an old pro," she said, smiling.

I nodded and looked back down at my magazine, still opened to the golf clubs. She'd think I was either a slow reader or a serious golf fanatic.

What I didn't tell her was that although I made this trip every summer, I'd never actually gone without my older sister. But that was none of her business. Let her think I flew alone all the time, between golf games.

"Your daddy must be so excited," the flight attendant said.

As if I still called him Daddy! Give me a break! But I wondered if he *was* excited. He wouldn't jump around hooting like a kid, of course, so it would be hard to tell.

When we hit turbulence, my gut lurched to my throat and I clutched the armrests. I heard one lady gasp and a girl squeak. The man beside me calmly typed along with no expression on his face. I guess he didn't think we were going to plummet to the ground and shatter in flaming bits on impact. Had he noticed me grab the armrests? I hoped I hadn't squeaked like that girl. I relaxed my hands, emptied my face of expression, and made sure my eyes didn't bug out at the next roll of the plane.

The flight was l-o-n-g. I couldn't see the movie over the seat in front of me—but it was a stupid movie I'd already seen twice anyway. And the meal was gluey clumps of yuck. It was a relief to look out the window and finally see the gray expanse of Dadland (as Liz and I called it).

They must be having another drought, I thought, because there was nothing green below the layer of smog—just an endless spread of buildings, roads, and freeways.

I reminded myself not to panic if Dad wasn't there, but the thought made my heart pound anyway. He'd been late the year before last and it had worked out okay. But my sister, Liz, had been with me. She was fourteen then.

Well, if Dad's not there, I told myself, I'll just go down to baggage claim, get my suitcase, and wait for him outside. I tried to imagine doing all that without freaking out. I wouldn't know what kind of car to watch for, because Dad changed cars all the time, so I'd just have to stand on the curb near the shuttle buses until he honked or waved or something.

I wondered if Dad would be alone. Last year his girlfriend Bobbie was with him when he came to get us. Boy, Liz was ticked about that. She'd hated Bobbie's guts, instantly and completely.

I triple-checked to make sure I had my baggage claim ticket as we pulled up to gate C-3.The same flight attendant offered to check my overhead compartment. She must've thought I was too short to reach it. I knew I could ask her to help me find baggage claim and all that. But on second thought, I'd rather get lost.

I filed down the tube into the waiting area. It was huge and crowded and hard to focus on. Then I spotted Dad. Phew! He was shoving toward me. I suddenly wondered what to do. Shake hands? I'd *hated* having to hug my crying mom in front of all those strangers at the gate back home.

Dad thumped me on the back, hard. "Hey, Big Guy!" he said. Then he mussed up my hair.

I was definitely *not* a "Big Guy," but Dad had been calling me that forever.

"Hey, Dad," I said back.

Then we were sucked into the herd, mooing away from the gate. I felt good. I hadn't had to hug, I wouldn't have to handle the whole suitcase business myself, and I was alone with Dad.

It stank of exhaust outside the airport, and I patted my pocket, making sure my inhaler was there in case my asthma kicked up. We crossed to parking lot E. Dad was telling me that he was taking me somewhere special for lunch and that he hoped I was hungry. I was.

This year his car was a Porsche Boxster—a bright yellow two-seater with space in the back for a dog or tennis rackets.

If both Liz and I had come, I guess that would've been *my* seat.

Then we were off, moving past bleached-out buildings and billboards. At a red light, Dad said, "Watch this." He pushed a button and the car shuddered as the top went down and folded itself away.

"A convertible! Cool!" I said, blinking in the sudden glare, wishing I had sunglasses. Dad smiled past me. I looked over and saw a guy at a bus stop give us a thumbs-up. I bet he thought I was just some son out for a ride with his father— and he was right! For once it wasn't like when I'm with friends' dads and sort of hope people think they're mine.

"How's Liz?" Dad asked.

"She's good." I thought about saying more—maybe tell him about Liz's boyfriend, Jet, or something—but the traffic and wind were loud. Anyway, he didn't ask for details.

I wondered for the hundredth time what I'd say if Dad asked me why Liz hadn't come. I hoped I could get away with a shrug and an "I don't know."

When Liz had first told me she wasn't coming to California, I'd thought she just couldn't tear herself away from her boyfriend. But she'd said, "No, it has nothing to do with Jet. There's just no *room* for me in Dadland."

So then I'd thought she meant because Dad always had two-bedroom apartments and Liz felt way too old to share a room with me. But she'd shaken her head and said, "Every year I hope it'll be different. Like Dad will make time for us. And every year I'm disappointed. Who needs it?"

"But maybe this year *will* be different!" I'd argued.

"I hope so, John," Liz had said. "I hope you have a great time."

When Liz had called Dad, I'd secretly picked up the phone in Mom's room and listened in. Liz had come right out with it: "Dad, I won't be able to visit this summer."

Dad hadn't asked why. He'd just said, "Gee, that's too bad, Princess."

"John's still coming, though," she'd said. "Aren't you, John?"

Caught! How'd she know I was on the line? I'd been silent as death! "Uh—yeah," I'd stammered. "Sure I'm coming." Then I'd added a "Can't wait!"

And here I was. I looked over at my dad and he asked, "And your mother? How's she?"

"She's good too," I said over the roar.

He nodded, satisfied, I guess. If it had been Liz driving alone with him, I suppose he would have been satisfied by a "He's good" about me.

Dad gave the valet his car keys and led me into a restaurant. A woman with blonde hair was waiting at a table. When she saw us, she started to get up, but then sat back down.

As Dad steered me toward that woman's table, my gut sank. "Sorry we're late," he said, kissing her on the lips. "Cora, this is the Big Guy."

"Hi, John," Cora said. "It's great to finally meet you. I've heard *soooo* much about you."

I tried to smile, wondering if I was supposed to lie and say I'd heard about her too.

I looked at the menu. Wednesday's special was a cheese-burger. When I commented that it cost a gazillion times more than at McDonald's, Cora said that it would taste "at least a *gazillion* times better." She said *gazillion* like she thought it was the most hilarious word she'd ever heard.

We ordered, then waited forever for the food to come. Cora asked me some questions, like how my flight was, and whether I was enjoying summer vacation, but mostly she and Dad talked while I looked around. The restaurant was trying to seem old and shabby, but in a bright new way. The waiters wore neckties with pink flowers on them. Very L.A.

Dad looked the same as always—tan, tall, happy. I glanced at Cora and realized that her eyebrows weren't made of hair. They were *drawn* on. I wondered if she'd shaved off her real eyebrows or if she'd been born without them.

When the food came, Cora took a wad of gum out of her mouth, wrapped it in a tissue, and stuck it in her purse. How many gobs of gum did she have in there? I pictured her pulling her hand out and having gum glommed onto each fingertip, stretching like pizza cheese. Maybe her eyebrows had gotten caught in her gum!

"Oh!" Cora said, seeing me smile. "Wanna hear a cute joke, John?"

The word *cute* made me suspicious.

Cora cleared her throat, sat up straighter, and said, "Why don't cannibals eat clowns?"

"Why?" Dad asked.

"Because they taste funny!" Cora said, cracking up.

I wanted to groan, but Dad was smiling, so I smiled too. I wondered if I would've liked the joke more if someone else had told it.

The meal dragged on long after Dad and I had finished our burgers. Cora just kept pushing her food around, taking microscopic mouse nibbles now and then.

I was eager to see Dad's new apartment. He called it his "pool pad." A swim sounded great, and I was ready to go.

I looked at Dad and he winked at me. I hoped that meant he knew I was dying to leave, but when the waiter asked if he wanted more coffee, Dad said, "Sure."

"How was your burger?" Cora asked me.

I shrugged. "It was okay."

Finally, Dad pushed his chair back, fanned a bunch of twenty-dollar bills out on the table, and got up to leave. I jumped to my feet.

"Whoa there, Big Guy!" Dad said. "I've got to get to a meeting. Cora has graciously taken the afternoon off—just to help us out." He and Cora exchanged smiles. Then Dad said, "She'll run you back to the apartment for me and I'll meet you there later. Fair enough?"

I sat back down, smiled as if it were no big deal, and said, "Fair enough." I should've gotten an Oscar for *that* performance!

Cora finished her coffee. "Your father's quite a guy," she gushed. "You're a lucky boy."

I cranked out another smile.

She stuck a fresh stick of gum in her mouth and offered me one—which I declined.

"He was so excited about your visit," she said. "That's *all* he could talk about."

I tried to believe her.

"It was so cute how worried he was about what you'd want to do while you were here. He was scared you'd be bored and all that. It was sweet."

That's when I knew she was totally full of it. No way would Dad worry about stuff like that.

Cora said she didn't have any small bills to tip the valet, so I had to lend her two dollars to get her car back. Then she turned on the car radio and out came *Muzak*. She didn't gag or retch or even change the station! She hummed along, cracking her gum. Sheesh.

chapter two

We parked underground, and Cora led me up a flight of stairs. When we got to the top, she punched a number code to unlock the door. She knew it by heart. The door opened on a U-shaped courtyard surrounding a swimming pool.

We walked along a balcony corridor. There was only one person out. He was leaning over the railing, right in our way. When he saw us, he grinned and said, "Hey, John. How ya doing?" I was confused. How'd this kid know my name?

"John, this is Beau Lubeck," Cora said, as if that explained everything.

"What took you so long?" Beau asked with a goofy smile. "I thought your plane came in at noon!"

Cora answered for me. "We stopped for lunch at the *Ivy!*" The way she said it, I could tell it was supposed to be a hot spot.

"Cool," Beau said, nodding. He and Cora obviously knew

each other, and Beau clearly knew way more about me than I knew about him—which was easy, of course, since I knew *zip* about him.

I watched the numbers on the doors we passed. I knew Dad's apartment was 216 because I'd sent him a Father's Day card. Sure enough, that's where Cora stopped. She took out a key and opened the door. I wondered whether it was her own key or Dad had lent it to her for today.

Beau loped inside right along with us. He was taller than me—no surprise there—but he looked about my age. He showed me the guest room, where I was going to sleep.

Then the kitchen. He opened the fridge and said, "There's never anything in here." From there he went back to the living room, clicked on the TV, and started listing off the cable channels we could get. He said *we* as if he lived here. Did he? Did Cora? Was Beau Cora's son? They didn't look alike. Beau was long and bony. Cora was sort of round and springy-looking. If they both fell off the balcony, I thought, Beau would shatter and Cora would bounce.

Beau was still telling me about the apartment. Something about the elevator not working. Cora took off her shoes and picked up a magazine. She chewed her gum with her mouth open. I hate that.

"Wanna go swimming?" Beau asked me.

That's when I realized my suitcase was still in Dad's car.

"No sweat," Beau said. "I can lend you a suit."

I didn't want to borrow this kid's trunks; I was sure I'd look dorky in them. But it was hot and I really wanted to swim. I also wanted to see where Beau kept his clothes. At least I'd find out if he lived here. I couldn't *ask,* because then he'd know I didn't know squat about who Dad lives or doesn't live with. So I said okay.

Beau bolted out the door.

Cora looked up from her magazine and said, "Beau lives a few doors down. It'll just take him a second." One mystery solved.

"Can I use the phone?" I asked, remembering that I'd promised to call when I got in.

Cora giggled at me. "Of course you can! It's your phone!"

My phone? Yeah, I guessed since this was my dad's apartment, it was kinda mine too. "Where is it?"

Cora pointed to the coffee table right under her nose, but I didn't want to use *that* phone. I hesitated, then asked, "Is there another one?"

"It's a cordless," Cora said, cracking her gum. "You can take it in another room if you need *privacy.*"

My sister, Liz, answered. "How's the Phantom?" she asked.

"He's at a meeting," I mumbled.

"Surprise, surprise," Liz said sympathetically. "Bobbie still around?"

"She has morphed into *Cora,*" I whispered. "She's here now."

Liz groaned. "Well, be brave," she said. "Here's Mom."

"Be brave about *what*?" Mom asked, instantly alarmed.

"Nothing."

"I was expecting your call *hours* ago! Is everything okay?"

I rolled my eyes. Mom—always ready to worry.

After I'd reassured Mom that all was well, and promised to call her the next day, I changed into Beau's trunks. They were too big on me, of course, and I looked stupid. I was afraid I'd swim right out of them, but somehow they hung on, and the water felt great. I may not be so hot at stuff like basketball and soccer, but I can sure swim. Beau could go farther than me without taking a breath, but when we raced using no arms, then using no legs, I beat him both times.

While we were floating around between races, I asked Beau what grade he was in. He said, "Going into eighth." I told him I was going into seventh, and he didn't act snotty that I was younger. But maybe he already knew that from my dad.

Suddenly, a teenaged-looking guy in shorts came hauling down the stairs, ran to the far edge of the pool, and dove in. He swam underwater toward us, then dragged Beau under. It seemed way longer than a regular dunk before Beau popped to the surface, sputtering and cursing.

The kid swam back to the other end of the pool, leaving Beau clinging to the side with his chest heaving. When he had the wind, Beau called out, "You cretin!" But the other boy was already out of the pool and on his way upstairs. He didn't even turn around.

Beau looked at me and muttered, "My brother."

"Your *brother?*"

Beau nodded. "One of them," he said. "The ugly one." Then he smiled a half smile.

"He almost killed you," I said.

"Harsh fellow, that Eric," Beau agreed. "My folks say he's been trying to kill me since the day I was born." He shrugged as if it were no biggie. "I figure if he *really* wanted to kill me, he would've succeeded by now."

I laughed because Beau did.

Then I saw Dad leaning over the railing, waving down at me. Or at me and Beau. "Hey, guys!" he called.

"Hay is for horses," Beau called back. Dad laughed at that corny old line.

I started to climb out of the pool, but Dad put his hand up to stop me and said, "I'll just change and be right down."

This would be a good time for Beau to get lost, I thought. I'd been here for hours and still hadn't really seen my dad alone. But if Dad was bringing Cora down to the pool with him, it wouldn't matter whether Beau was gone or not. I clenched my fists, imagining a whole week with eyebrowless Cora. Liz may have hated Dad's girlfriend last year, but I thought Cora, with her key to Dad's apartment, and the way she planted herself down as if she owned the place, was way worse than Bobbie.

Dad came down—alone, thank goodness—wearing mirrored sunglasses and a robe over his bathing suit, looking like Mr. Hollywood. He was loaded with supplies: a drink with clinking ice, a newspaper, his cell phone. He scraped a chair over to one of the umbrellas and sat down. "How's the water?" he asked.

"Great!" I answered. "Come on in!"

"Maybe later," Dad said, dialing his phone.

"Liar!" Beau teased. Then he told me, "He's *never* put a toe in here. Not one toe!"

My face got hot. I didn't know my own father doesn't swim, but Beau did. Same as he knew what cable stations Dad got and that there wasn't anything in his fridge. And this Beau kid just called my dad a *liar* without batting an eye!

I was suddenly sick of swimming, but what was I supposed to do? Go sit under the umbrella with Dad? Go upstairs and hang around watching Cora chew gum? I sat on the edge of the pool.

"Race you with one arm and one leg," Beau offered.

"Nah, I'm just gonna sit awhile."

"You okay? You breathing okay?" Beau asked.

He knew about my *asthma?* My father had told this complete stranger about my *asthma?* I seethed with sudden hatred. I hated Beau. I wished his brother *had* drowned him.

"We've gotta go pretty soon," Dad called over to me—or to *us*; I couldn't tell.

"Go where?" I asked, hoping he meant just him and me.

"Cora's sister invited us to her birthday barbecue," Dad said. "Supposed to be there sixish."

I sighed. Cora. Why had I thought this trip would be any different than the rest? They'd all been nonstop busy, with some girlfriend always around.

I wished my sister was here. By now she would've grilled Cora and Beau and we'd know exactly how they fit into Dad's life. She'd also know that I felt like spit and she'd kid me out of it.

I remembered the plane ride home from our visit last year. When I'd said, "But we never really *saw* him," Liz had answered, "Phantom Father! Tune in next summer as the mystery continues!" And she had pulled her blanket up around her face like a Dracula cape.

chapter three

Beau hauled himself out of the pool and grabbed his towel. "When are you gonna be back?" he asked.

Dad shrugged. "Late, probably."

Beau nodded, and I hated him a little less because he wasn't coming with us. He pointed a foot at me and said, "So, what are you doing tomorrow?"

I looked at Dad.

"I'll be in meetings all morning," Dad said. "I guess you guys could go to the beach or something."

By ourselves? I wondered. Just me and Beau? I could picture the expression on my mom's face.

Beau sprawled on a lounge chair with his towel over his head, and Dad gathered up all his stuff and led me upstairs. Cora wasn't in the apartment, and I was glad. Now maybe Dad and I could . . . do whatever it is boys and their dads do. Talk? Play chess? Tell dirty jokes?

Then Dad turned on the TV and his computer. I'd forgotten that he does that. Liz used to say that Dad surrounded himself with monitors so he could bask in their glow. That was back when she was calling him "Dr. *Raaay* from Outer *Spaaace.*"

It's true that it's impossible to imagine Dad living in a pre-screen era, like the Old West or ancient Egypt. But computers are his work, so he's *supposed* to care about them. And I think he just liked the television on all the time for company.

I guess my company wasn't enough.

I stood around feeling odd and goose-bumpy. I wondered if Dad felt at all shy or whatever too. But I decided that idea made precisely zero sense.

"Here's your room, Big Guy," he called from the doorway to the guest room. He tossed me a towel.

I took a long, long shower. Then I admitted to myself that I was kind of hiding, and I got out. I unpacked my junk and got dressed. Then I stood around. I hated feeling so *stiff!* I'd been dying to come here. Dying to get out of my all-girl house. My mom, my sister—even my dog, Ditz, was a girl!

Ditz. If she were here, she'd put her head in my lap and look at me with those big eyes of hers, her wagging tail banging into everything.

This is stupid! I thought. Here I am in Dad's bachelor apartment with Dad—who thinks I'm old enough to go to the beach by myself—and I'm wishing I were with *Ditz?*

I walked out of the room and said, "Hey, Dad."

He smiled back. "Hey, Big Guy."

"So what's the story with Cora and Beau?" I asked, casual, cool.

Dad started to answer but the phone rang. I sat down in front of the TV while he talked. It was one of those shows where contestants scream their heads off and try to see who can act like a bigger jerk. One guy was balancing stuff on his head, including some yellow slime that glopped him when it fell. I hoped it wasn't my dad's favorite program.

Dad hung up. "We're outta here!" he said, grabbing his wallet, keys, and beeper. "Cora will be in a lather if we're late."

But when we got to Cora's, she wasn't even ready. Her apartment was girly, with breakable stuff all over the place. I sank into her flowery couch and almost drowned in cushions. Dad chose a more reasonable chair. He picked up a magazine and flicked through the pages, his foot tapping.

My eyes started to itch, then water. I sneezed. Sneezed again. "Dad?" I said. "Does Cora have a cat?"

"Four," he said without looking up.

The thing about allergies and asthma is, after you've had a few attacks, you start to panic at the *idea* of an attack. At least I do. I mean, just looking at a *picture* of a cat can make me wheezy. I got up and said, "I'm gonna wait outside."

Dad followed me out the door. "Sorry, Big Guy," he said. "I forgot."

"That's okay," I said, embarrassed. I felt my pockets. Dang! I'd forgotten my inhaler! If a picture of a cat can make me wheezy, knowing I don't have my inhaler can make it ten times worse.

I told myself to calm down. I'd been in that cat house only a couple of minutes. Maybe I didn't need the inhaler. I breathed in, out. All was well.

Four? I thought. Why would a person need *four* cats?

My dad—who'd never wheezed a wheeze, who'd probably never even had a cold—was looking down, way down, at his short weakling of a son, with an expression of . . . what? Pity?

"Really, Dad," I said, doing my best to smile. "I'm fine."

Cora came out and Dad said, "Some father I am, eh? I forgot than John's allergic to cats."

"I'm *fine,*" I said again.

Cora nodded at me. Then, taking Dad's arm, she smiled up all lovey-dovey at him, and said, "John's perfectly fine and you're a *perfectly* wonderful father. Now, let's go!"

She had lipstick on one of her front teeth.

Back home a barbecue means ribs or burgers—or chicken, at least—and corn or potatoes. Not this one. This one meant tiny snacks being whisked over my head by waitresses wearing matching T-shirts. At first, Dad introduced me to people. Then he got involved in conversations and I was left standing around feeling awkward and hungry.

One lady tried to entertain me with dumb questions like, How'd I like California, and Had I seen any movie stars yet?

Two people asked me if I knew Iris. Last year, some friend of Dad's thought it was hilarious that Liz and I didn't know a Santa Ana was a wind. In California they name the *wind* and expect everyone else to know that. I figured *Iris* was another California in-joke. So I just smiled—the dolt son from Kansas who doesn't even know what *Iris* is!

Then a woman grabbed my hand, saying, "You'll be bored to death out here with us old fogies." She dragged me indoors.

It turned out Iris was an actual girl, and we found her in the kitchen, looking guilty. But the woman who dragged me there didn't notice. "Iris, this is Matt's son, John," she said. "Here all the way from Kansas!"

Iris half-smiled. Her mouth was full, and she was hiding her hands behind her back. She was taller than me. Not much, but still.

The woman walked away.

After Iris swallowed, she said, "And your little dog Toto too?"

That was another California thing. All they knew about Kansas was that Dorothy came from there in *The Wizard of Oz*.

"Actually, my dog's name is Ditz," I said.

"Ditz? As in, Boy, is she a ditz?"

"Yeah."

"That's a ditzy name." She giggled. "But my hamster's name is Puff Ball, so maybe I shouldn't judge."

"What were you doing?" I asked.

"Huh?"

"When we came in."

Iris giggled again, then showed me her hands, sticky red

with goo. "Caught me red-handed!" she howled. "I hate the powder on the outside." Then I noticed the mess next to her. She'd been squeezing the jelly out of the little doughnuts on the dessert tray.

"Powdered sugar makes me sneeze," I agreed. "It's like sweet dust."

She handed me one. I looked around. "Don't worry, we won't get in trouble," Iris said. "I live here."

So I sucked the jelly out of the doughnut the way she did. Not bad. Then she asked if I wanted to see the new Mac she'd gotten for her birthday. I asked when her birthday was and she said, "Last Thursday. I'm a Leo. What are you?"

I couldn't remember.

Iris rolled her eyes. "Well, when's your birthday?" she asked. "We can look it up."

"May," I told her.

"I think that's Gemini," she said, leading me to her room. "How old are you?"

I wanted to say fourteen, but I figured she wouldn't believe me. "Twelve," I admitted to her back.

"Me too," she said. And I breathed with relief.

Iris turned on her computer and talked constantly while searching for a game we both liked. I sneaked peeks at her room. I hadn't been in a girl's bedroom, beside my sister's, since I was a little kid. But Iris's room didn't reveal any girl secrets. It was pretty much a regular room except for the stuffed animals.

Then Iris stopped talking and leaned closer to me. For a

split second I thought she was going to kiss me! I held my breath. But then she just whispered, "So what's the inside scoop? Is your dad *serious* about Aunt Cora?"

"Sh-she's your aunt?" I stammered, caught off guard. Then realized, *Duh,* Dad said we were going to Cora's sister's barbecue, so Iris was Cora's sister's kid.

"Does that mean yes or no?"

"Huh?"

"Well, is he going to propose or what?"

The meaning of her words finally dawned on me. "Propose *marriage?*" I asked.

"Oh," Iris said. "I guess that means no."

"No, it doesn't—I mean, not necessarily."

"You're being shady," Iris said. "I don't like that in a person." She crossed her arms, poked out her lower lip, and pretended to pout.

I didn't want to tell this girl that I had no idea what my dad planned to do about her aunt Cora or *anything* else. Iris probably thought normal sons know these things about their fathers. That fathers and sons *talk* about stuff.

Iris squinted at me. "Are you sworn to secrecy?"

I shrugged.

"Aha! You're honor-bound by your word. Sticking to your promise, even under torture. I like that in a person!"

Eventually, Dad and Cora found me and said it was time to head out. I wondered if I'd see Iris again. I liked her—even though her good-bye was "Follow the Yellow Brick Road!"

By the time we'd dropped Cora back at her apartment, and gotten stuck in traffic (it's always rush hour in L.A.), and climbed the stairs to number 216, I could barely keep my eyes open. I went to the guest room and crashed. One day down, six to go.

chapter four

"Morning, Big Guy," Dad said when I stumbled into the kitchen the next day. "Hungry?"

He was drenched, his T-shirt stuck to him. A drop of sweat hung off the tip of his nose.

"You still run every day?" I asked.

"Five miles, rain or shine," he said, opening the fridge. "Let's see, we've got eggs and we've got eggs. Or, you could have a couple of eggs. What do you think?"

I smiled. "I think I'll have eggs."

"Good choice," Dad said, and began cracking and cooking. "I've got a nine o'clock," he said, "that should be done by ten-thirty, eleven at the latest. And a . . ." He leaned over and peered down at his planner. "Oh," he said, "a one-thirty that could run to, say, three. Maybe I can stop by here in between, depending. You going to be all right till maybe fourish?"

I was stumped. Be all right doing what? Sitting here in the apartment for seven and a half hours?

"Sure," I said anyway.

"You've got my pager number and Cora's number and a key over there by the phone. Oh, and the combination for the outside door is thirty-three, twelve, nineteen."

I looked around for a pen. "Thirty-three what?"

He repeated it. Then he had to repeat it again because the pen didn't work.

"Not much to eat in the house, I'm afraid," Dad said. "But there are restaurants up on Grand."

I had no idea where *Grand* was. I'd never even been in this neighborhood before. "Well," I said, trying to sound calm, "there's always eggs."

"Over easy—the way you like them," he said proudly, placing my plate in front of me.

No, I thought, that's Liz. I'm the one who likes them scrambled dry.

"Aren't you having any?" I asked.

"I'll pick up something on the way," Dad said, heading for the bathroom. Soon I heard him singing in the shower.

I ate my eggs, or Liz's eggs, looking around, imagining myself there all day. The only magazines Dad got were *Forbes* and *Business Week*. I knew I'd go into a coma of boredom reading them. There was also TV. One in the kitchen, a bigger one in the living room. Probably one in Dad's bedroom too.

The phone rang. I wondered if I should answer. Then I thought, I'm his *son!* Sons answer their fathers' phones! I'd never think twice about answering *Mom's*.

"Who's this?" the voice asked.

"This is John. Matt's son," I said.

"No kidding! I didn't even know he _had_ a son!"

What could I say to _that_?

"Well," the voice went on, "your dad around?"

"He's in the shower."

"Tell him Chris called, okay?"

I hoped Chris wasn't a good friend.

And then, in a rush of sports jacket and briefcase, Dad was gone and it was very, very quiet.

It's not like I was never in the house alone at home. Mom worked. My sister, especially since she'd met Jet, was out all the time. But at home—well, I was _home!_ I had my stuff. I had my life. There was Ditz. There was food in the fridge.

Dad always had a million appointments and meetings, but Liz had been with me all the other visits, and she's four years older. Well, I thought, time to grow up! I hated it that my mom babied me so much at home, so I should be _thrilled_ now, right?

The first thing I did was try to go back to bed, but my eyes wouldn't close. So I got dressed and started poking around the guest room. My friend Theo had divorced parents, but he didn't call his room in either of their houses a "guest" room.

Nothing in the drawers but some Kleenex and a few pens.

Bathroom next. Wow, Dad sure uses a lot of hair stuff. What was this? I unscrewed a cap and sniffed. _Dad!_ It was my father—in a bottle! Oops. I must've jumped because now I'd spilled Dad on my hand, my leg, the floor. As I wiped it up with great wads of toilet paper, I laughed at my own stupidity. *Of course* that dad-smell was some kind of cologne. Had I thought he smelled like that naturally? That his *sweat* smelled like that?

Now what? Flush the wad of dad-smelling toilet paper down the toilet and probably plug it up? Shove it in the garbage can and have it smell like Dad-in-trash?

I destroyed the evidence clump by clump, four flushes. When I went to crank open the window, I jumped *again!* A huge palm-tree head was bobbing there, made all wiggly and mysterious by the bathroom window's pocked-up privacy glass. Since I'd seen it out of the corner of my eye, I guess I thought it was someone watching me. One more jump and I figured I'd probably have a heart attack. Spies must have nerves of steel.

On to the kitchen. Boring—pots and pans, silverware, plates. A bottom drawer with a hammer and two screwdrivers and a few batteries.

It was as if no one lived there. Maybe my dad really *is* Dr. Ray from Outer Space, or a fugitive, I thought. And lives a secret life somewhere else. Maybe he just pretends to live here while I visit. It's a cover-up or something!

I knew it was stupid and criminal and whatnot for me to snoop around like that. I didn't even know exactly what I was looking for. Clues to the Phantom Father's real identity? Or maybe his diary full of pages and pages about how he missed his kids, especially me, and how he cursed the day he ever left us.

When my uncle Don found out he was dying, he wrote letters and made videos for his son, Davy, to read and watch one day when he grew up. I was definitely *not* jealous of my little cousin for having a dead father, but the letters would be okay, I thought.

I went into Dad's room. Closet first. Clothes, shoes. A box! I pulled it out and opened it. It was full of secret documents!

No, wait, they were electric bills, rent receipts, car payment stubs. Wow, that Porsche Boxster was *expensive!* And he was paying a fortune for this apartment too.

Beeeezzzz. An alarm! I shoved the box back into the closet. *Beeeezzzz.* I ran out of Dad's room, heart pounding, caught! Then I realized it was the door buzzer.

I could hear Mom's voice in my head, saying not to open the door to strangers. I looked through the fish-eye peephole and there was Beau, picking his nose.

By the time I got the door opened, both his hands were jammed into his pockets and he was smiling his goofy smile.

"What's up?" he asked.

"Nothing," I said, stepping aside to let him in.

"Dad gone?"

"If you mean *my* dad," I said, "yes, he is." Then I felt bad for sounding like such a twit. "Gone till about four," I added.

"So you wanna do something?"

I shrugged. "Like what?"

Beau shrugged back. "I dunno."

"Well, I don't know where I am," I said. "I mean like the neighborhood or what's around here."

"There's nothin'," Beau said.

"Oh."

"But I can give you the tour," he offered.

I shoved some money in my pocket, grabbed the key, the piece of paper with the outside door combination, and my inhaler, and said, "Let's go."

As we went down the stairs, I could hear someone running up from below. We turned the corner and there, coming at us, was Beau's brother Eric. He didn't say anything; he just smacked Beau on the side of his head as he passed. The sound of that smack echoed through the stairwell.

Beau made an *umph* sound and reeled for a second, then shook himself like a dog and continued down the stairs without comment.

When we got outside, he said, "The nothing on your left is the nonmarket. They don't sell anything. And over there is the nothing-repair where they don't fix stuff."

"I don't suppose they have gas at that gas station," I said, pointing.

"Nope," Beau said.

We passed a nail place, and Beau said that was where the local witches got their talons sharpened. Then he pretended to faint from the smell of incense that billowed out the door of a weird bookstore. His ear was still red from his brother's smack.

When we passed a dog-grooming place, I thought of Ditz. "My dog weighs sixty-five pounds," I said. "But when we take her to the groomer, she crinches down, making herself as small as she can, hoping they won't notice her."

Beau laughed. "I've never had a dog," he said. "Just brothers." Then he pointed across the street, saying, "Hey, if you're not hungry, we can go to the anti-diner, where they don't have anything to eat. Want to?"

"Nah," I said. "I'm starved."

Beau grinned and punched my arm. A little too hard, but still.

The diner was one of those red-and-white places that have old Coke ads all over the walls for decoration. There's one in the mall near my house.

Beau ordered eggs over easy, and I wondered if *he* was the one my dad confused me with instead of Liz. Did Dad make eggs for Beau?

Sitting still like that, indoors, I suddenly realized I stank. Phew! All that spilled cologne had formed a cloud around me. I smelled like Ultra-Mega-Dad. My father times ten.

Beau didn't say anything or fan the air or faint, but I bet he noticed. How could he *not*? I almost told him about my cologne-spilling event, but then he'd know that I'd been snooping in Dad's bathroom—and that would sound so lame and pathetic.

I ordered a tuna melt and Beau said, "You like those too? Just like your old man!"

"My dad likes tuna melts?" I asked. Another thing Beau knew that I didn't.

"Now, *my* dad, on the other hand," Beau said, sprinkling salt on the tabletop, "is a tofu dude. He won't even come in here 'cause he's afraid the preservatives and toxic animal fats will get him." Beau grabbed his own neck and wrestled with himself.

When he was finished, he licked his finger and dipped it into the salt. "Me," he said, "I'm a whatever-I-can-shove-in-my-mouth kind of guy." And he licked the salt off his fingers.

I was starting to like Beau. At least, I could see why Dad liked him. I wanted to ask him about *his* dad, and I wanted to ask about *mine,* but instead I said, "Are we near the beach?"

"No. We're not anywhere near anything. Like I say, we are *nowhere!*"

"But yesterday my dad said . . ."

"We'd have to take the bus, or hitch a ride or something."

"Is it far?"

"Everything's far. But I couldn't go today anyway. I gotta stick around. Help with the boys."

I didn't know what he meant, but our food came. I ate my second meal of the day and it was only nine-thirty.

After we ate, we roamed around. Beau wasn't kidding: There was nothing there. Just the usual video stores and coffee places. But it was less boring because it was all so Californian—that sunlight that's a whole different color than back home and those weird plants that make our plants seem blah.

Then Beau suddenly slumped down and nudged me. I followed his eyes, and there on the corner were a bunch of girls. I straightened up as tall as I could while Beau, who actually *is* tall, made himself shorter.

The girls were ignoring us pretty hard and tossing their hair around. Beau dragged his feet, kicking at nothing. Then he horked up a huge mouthful and spit a perfect gob. He was an even more impressive spitter than my friend Theo, and that was saying something.

One girl shrieked, "Ewwww, gross!" And they all started to giggle like crazy, throwing their hair around even more. Then Beau and I bumped into each other and, like a klutz, I stumbled off the sidewalk. My arm just barely touched a cactus and, *ouch!*, I was cut and bleeding.

"It'll probably swell up," Beau said, darting a glance at the girls. "Harsh, angry vegetable. Has some kind of poison."

"Poison?" I asked, wondering if I was allergic. Great, I thought. Now I'll break out in hives and start to wheeze right in front of everyone. How manly.

Just then a van pulled up. All the girls piled into it and were whisked away. Beau and I watched them disappear.

Then I looked at the spiky plant that had stabbed me. It had thorns and a giant asparagus-looking thing poking up in the middle.

"It's an Eric plant," Beau said. "Just being ugly isn't enough. Gotta be *mean* too."

I waited for the swelling to start and my breath to cut off, wondering if I'd have to hightail it to the hospital. But the cut just acted like any old cut, and my inhaler did not have to leave my pocket.

I pointed at one of those bright pink bushes that climb up

walls. "My sister hates these," I told Beau. "Last summer she told them to shut up and stop screaming at her."

Beau nodded. "Pushy plant, bougainvillea."

Liz hated all the California plants last year. She'd said they were all show-offs. I think it was because Dad's girlfriend Bobbie was sort of a show-off and Liz had lumped her and everything else about California into one heap. It hadn't been our best visit to Dadland. But then, maybe none of them were.

chapter five

On our way back Beau slapped himself on the forehead, spun on his heels, and said, "I was supposed to get milk."

We walked back to a little market we'd passed earlier, and Beau picked out a weird carton. "Soy milk. Untouched by cow," he said when I asked him what it was.

The clerk, who had a braided beard, knew Beau by name. Beau told him he'd spent all the milk money on breakfast, and the guy told him he could pay next time. I tried to imagine that happening back home. Impossible. I'd been going to the same store for a hundred years and no one there ever recognized me. Maybe I was just more forgettable than Beau.

"His Royal Ugliness used to be a stock boy here," Beau said as we left. "They fired his pimply butt."

"Why?" I asked, imagining Eric smacking the customers in the head.

Beau shrugged. "He can't be bothered with anything but his music, so he hardly ever showed up. Good thing they don't think all Lubecks are created equal. They say they're gonna hire me one of these days, for after school and weekends. That'll sure beat my job this summer."

"What job?" I asked.

"Baby-sitting," he said, and for one sickening second I wondered if Beau meant baby-sitting *me!* Could my dad have hired Beau to hang out with me?

But then Beau said, "My ma pays me to help out."

Baby-sitting *Eric?* I didn't get the joke and felt dumb. I hate that.

We climbed the stairs of our building and Beau went into apartment 212 to change into his swim trunks. Now I knew where he lived. I wondered if he shared a room with Eric. If Beau's apartment was like my dad's, it had only two bedrooms.

Uh-oh, I must've forgotten to close Dad's apartment door. It was wide open! Mom was always ragging on me for stuff like that. But when I walked in, there was my dad on the phone.

He saw me and hung up fast. "Where were you?" he demanded, shaking a finger at me. "You didn't even leave a blasted note! I almost called the police!"

"But I thought . . . I thought you said . . . ," I stammered.

"And why didn't you tell me Chris called? That was an important—a *very* important message!"

"Well, I, I'm sorry, I just . . ."

"Listen, mister," Dad said, "if this visit is going to work out, you're going to have to be *a lot* more responsible and considerate."

"I will. I just thought . . ."

"How do you think it sounded when your mother called and I had to say I had no idea where you were? What did that make *me* look like? Huh?"

"Mom called?" I asked, shocked. Mom *never* called here, ever! She'd made me promise about ninety times that *I'd* call *her* every day.

Dad's mouth clamped shut. He stopped shaking his finger at me and straightened up.

"Mom called *here*?" I asked again.

"Yeah, well," Dad said, suddenly quiet.

"Why?" I asked.

"Well, she . . ." Dad's eyes darted around. "I've got to get to my meeting. You leave a note if you're going out, okay, Big Guy?" He mussed my hair on his way out the door, then he turned and said, "Give your mother a call. I'll be back around six. We'll get some dinner."

Six? What happened to fourish? I wondered.

Beau appeared in the doorway, looking embarrassed. "Should I pretend I didn't hear all that?" he asked.

I shrugged like it was no biggie. "I gotta make a call."

"John?" Mom said in a very strange voice. "You okay?"

"Yeah."

"Johnny, honey . . ." There was a long pause. "Liz doesn't think I should tell you until you get home, but I don't think that's right."

"Tell me what?"

"We have bad news, son. Oh, Johnny, it's so sad. Will you be all right? Is your father there with you?"

"What is it?" I nearly yelled.

"He has a right to know," Mom said, and I figured she was talking to Liz. I heard my mom sob.

Then there was a scuffle sound. My sister's voice came on the phone. "She went after a car. You know how she does— just out of nowhere . . . Oh, John, Ditz is dead."

That wasn't true. That couldn't be true.

"She just shot out the door and there was no time to . . ." Liz was crying now. "It was so fast!"

Ditz wasn't dead. Why was Liz saying that? I don't know what else we said before hanging up.

I stood looking at the phone, but it seemed unreal—like a painting of a phone. And I felt far away from those voices who'd been crying. Light-years from what they'd said about Ditz. I don't know how long I stood there.

I finally left the kitchen. Beau was channel surfing. *He* didn't look particularly real either. "What's up?" he asked.

"Nothing," I said, and walked past him to the guest room. I got my trunks out of the drawer. I felt like I was moving in slow motion, as if the air in the room had turned thick and I had to push through it.

I changed. Put my clothes on the chair. Got a towel. Went

step by step out the door and down the stairs. Nothing looked right. The sun was too bright. The water in the pool was too blue. I looked back. Beau was bounding after me like a dog. Like Ditz. Leggy and eager and dumb.

I dove in. Sank to the bottom.

It's all my fault, I thought. Ditz didn't understand about vacations. She didn't know I was coming back; she only knew I was gone. Maybe she'd run out to go look for me! Maybe she'd thought I was in the car she'd chased.

I shouldn't have left her. And I should have trained her. The vet *told* me to work with her. He said if I just practiced a few minutes a day, she'd learn not to bolt out the door or run in the street or chase cars. Why didn't I?

I wasn't crying. Was it even possible to cry underwater? Then I realized my lungs were about to burst and I swam to the surface.

The chlorine in the pool probably made my eyes just as red as crying would. It would make a good camouflage, I thought. But there were no tears coming anyway. I swam lap after lap, waiting for the sense of Ditz to reach me, but it was as if her death were scrambled and my guts couldn't decode it.

That's good, I thought. I don't want to be a street weeper like Mom—willing to worry and cry anywhere, anytime. But I also didn't want to be taken by surprise later in front of anyone. Better to get it over with now.

So I made myself picture Ditz last fall when we brought her home from the Humane Society.

I'd always wanted a dog, but Mom had said no because of

my allergies. Then, right after I got home from Dadland last year, my doctor said that poodles are usually okay.

A poodle? Yecch! I pictured it all sissy-looking with bows. Figures I'd have to get a dorky dog instead of a *real* one, I thought.

Dr. Wong must've seen that I was bummed because he said, "The reason poodles are less allergy causing is that they don't shed. Their hair has to be cut, like ours. But they don't *have* to be cut goofy, you know. The pom-pom style is optional." And I felt much better.

I called the Humane Society every day until they finally had a puppy that was a poodle mix. Mom drove me over there, fretting out loud the whole way.

Then we saw Ditz. Tiny black Ditz.

I shoved my face into her fur, let her lick me, rubbed my eyes. Dr. Wong had said to do everything I *wasn't* supposed to do with cats, as a test.

Then we went home and I didn't wash my face or hands. Hoping, hoping. Mom watched me closely. No red eyes, no rash, no sneezing, no wheezing!

Liz came with us the next day for test number two. Dr. Wong had told me to do it twice, to be sure.

Ditz was so wiggly and excited, I could tell she remembered me. "She's sure no genius," Liz said when Ditz peed on her shoe. "In fact, she's a total *ditz!*" And the name stuck.

Still no tears. Eventually, I couldn't swim another stroke. I got out of the pool and lay on one of the deck chairs. I'd forgotten all about Beau, but there he was, floating on his back, eyes closed.

As much as I'd *wanted* to cry in the pool, I did *not* want to cry on land. Especially in front of Dad's friend Beau—the boy who my dad probably wished was his real son. What father *wouldn't* want Beau for his son? Beau was tall and friendly and funny. Does any man, when he has a kid, say, Gee, I hope he grows up short and unathletic! Please, God, make my son asthmatic and wimpy?

Then I wondered if Dad knew why Mom had called. Could he have known about Ditz and not told me?

Beau splashed me, shaking water out of his hair, then plopped down on the lounge chair next to mine. I turned to him and said, "My dog's dead." I heard my own words, but they sounded unreal, and I wondered if he'd think I was lying.

Beau blinked at me and his cheeks blotched up. Then his eyes got bloodshot. Wow! Could he just *do* that whenever he wanted to? Was he faking? I wondered. Making fun of me?

"Sorry," he said, wiping snot on his arm. "What kind of dog?"

"Mutt," I said. "Standard poodle, mostly. Black." Then I remembered the white spot under her chin, and I felt myself gag, as if my throat were being twisted.

"I never should've left," I mumbled.

"Huh?" Beau asked.

"She's my dog," I explained. But Beau still looked blank,

so I added, "She's *my* dog. I'm responsible for her. *Was* responsible for her."

"I dunno," Beau said. "When your number's up, your number's up. Right?"

I shrugged on the outside, but on the inside I screamed, *"No!"* Ditz was still a puppy; she hadn't even *picked* a number yet.

chapter six

"Are you hungry?" Beau asked, changing the subject.

"I'm always hungry," I said.

"Same here."

We went up to Beau's apartment. Beau's mom was on the couch right inside the door. She had lots of dark hair, curling all over the place. Beau said, "This is my mom." Then he introduced me by saying, "Mom, this is John. His dog got killed today, back in Kansas."

"Oh, I'm so sorry to hear that, John," Beau's mom said.

I nodded.

Then Beau said, "And that's baby Marcel."

It wasn't until that moment that I realized Beau's mom had a baby in her arms—and that the baby was *nursing!* Right in front of me! And I could even see some skin. Worse, I heard slurpy noises that must have been the baby drinking!

I didn't know what to say or where to look. I'd never been so embarrassed in my life, and I could barely hear what Beau's mother was saying to me. Something about food, but *yecch!* My appetite was permanently ruined.

I stumbled into the kitchen after Beau, and I just *knew* my eyeballs were hanging out on threads. But Beau didn't seem to notice or even care that I had seen what I had just seen! If someone caught *my* mother doing something like that, I'd die for sure.

Beau was pulling things out of cupboards and the fridge and piling the table with food. Gradually, I realized that maybe my appetite wasn't gone forever after all.

We sat down at the kitchen table to a feast of cold chicken, leftover spaghetti, olive bread that was bitter but okay with butter, and some yogurt-garlic-cucumber stuff that tasted way better than it sounds. Just as I was reaching for seconds, a completely naked kid came waddling into the kitchen. It was a boy; *that* was clear. And bigger than the baby in the living room. Their apartment was crammed with boys.

The kid climbed right up on Beau's lap. "This is Claude," Beau said. "Claude, this is John."

"Low," Claude said, which I guessed was baby talk for hello. Then Claude reached into Beau's plate and helped himself to a fistful of spaghetti. That killed my appetite once and for all.

"You got brothers and sisters?" Beau asked me, tipping his glass so Claude could drink, leaving a slimy spaghetti ring.

"A sister," I said. "Older."

Beau hit himself on the forehead. "Of course. *Liz!* Drama club, lead in the school play, right?"

"Right."

"Yeah, your dad says she's really talented."

"How would he know?" I mumbled. "He's never seen her act."

"Yeah, well, my dad's never heard me play tuba," Beau said.

"You play *tuba?*"

"No," Beau said, laughing. "Ha! Got you!"

I shook my head, watching Claude smear spaghetti all over his naked belly.

Beau's mom came into the kitchen. Her shirt was in place, thank goodness. She said, "Shhhhh! I finally got Marcel down for his nap." Then she asked me, in a whisper, what Dad and I had planned for my vacation.

I know grown-ups ask things just to ask them—without expecting real answers. But this time I said, "If it's like all my other trips, the plan is that my dad works all the time and stays busy. And I either tag along, bored to death, or sit and wait, bored to death."

Beau's mom burst out laughing. Then Beau did, then I did too. But for a few seconds my laugh sort of took off without me and I was afraid it would turn lunatic. That happens to me sometimes with Liz. She calls it the *screaming meemies.* Mom calls it hysterics. In either case, I call it something not to do in a stranger's kitchen.

Then Eric came in and loomed over the table, surveying

the remains of our lunch. He ripped off a hunk of bread and shoved it in his mouth without saying anything. He wasn't ugly, I realized—at least not on the outside. Actually, he looked a lot like Beau.

Eric grabbed a chicken leg and his mom said, "Sit down like a human being." She got up and handed him a plate. Then she looked at Beau and said, "You're on Claude duty."

Beau nodded. He carried Claude to the kitchen sink and wiped the spaghetti off him. Then I followed Beau and Claude outside. The kid still didn't have a stitch of clothes on. Everything about this place was wacky.

We leaned over the balcony railing and tried to toss gravel from the flowerpots into the pool. Beau missed as often as I did. Claude threw gravel too, and thought it was hilarious until some hit him on the head and he started to howl. Beau scooped him up and jiggled him until he started giggling again.

Then harmonica music started wailing out of Beau's apartment.

"He's going to wake the baby!" Beau spat, looking disgusted.

"Who?" I asked.

"His Ugliness."

"He's pretty good," I said.

"Not as good as he thinks he is," Beau said. "He thinks he's the new Chet Carter."

I nearly choked. "The new *who?*"

"Chet Carter, a blues harpist. That's another word for a harmonica." Beau put Claude down, bare butt on the cement. "You probably never heard of him."

"I know what a harp is," I said. "And I *know* Chet Carter. I didn't realize he was famous all the way out here! I thought he was sort of a Kansas thing."

Beau looked at me. "He's Eric's god."

"Well," I said, starting to laugh, "he's my friend Theo's *father!*"

"Get out!" Beau said.

"For real! Whenever he's not off recording or on tour, he takes me and Theo and this other friend of ours, Brad, bowling."

"You're kidding," Beau said. "Chet Carter bowls?"

I nodded.

"You've been *bowling* with Chet Carter? Eric will flip!"

"Eric ip!" Claude chirruped.

Then out of the apartment came a wail that was louder than the harp. *"Waaaaaa!"* Beau nodded an I-told-you-so nod, and Claude said, "Arcel!" which must've meant Marcel.

"Watch Claude a second," Beau said, and he ducked into the apartment. I looked down at Claude and my heart started to hammer. I'd never been alone with a little kid before. What if he suddenly took a flying leap down the stairs or over the railing? It would be my fault. I stuck my arms out to block him in case he was planning any quick moves. And I guess my eyes were bugging out, because Claude looked up and bugged *his* eyes back at me. Then he cracked up. It turns out it's pretty humiliating to be laughed at by a naked squirt.

Better laughing than crying, I told myself. Then, panicking, I wondered what I was supposed to do if he *did* start crying. No way was I going to pick him up and get peed on or worse. There was no telling if he was loaded. What was taking Beau so long, for Pete's sake?

Finally, Beau showed up and I was off duty. I practically danced with relief. Then Beau chased Claude around and wrestled him into shorts and shoes. It all seemed like way too much work, and I was grateful that my mom had quit having kids after me.

"I gotta take Mr. Claude to the park," Beau said. "Wanna come?"

I shrugged.

"Little kids are real chick magnets," Beau said. "You'll see." Then he batted his eyelashes and raised his voice in imitation of a girl: "Oh, he's *soooo* cute!"

So I went with them. A few old men were there playing cards, but there were no girls—not one. Beau pushed Claude on the swing. I thought about Ditz. She loved parks.

Whenever Beau stopped pushing the swing for half a second, Claude kicked his stubby legs and hollered. And if Beau dared to speak to me instead of paying total attention to him, Claude threw a fit. I wanted to clock him one. I didn't know how Beau could stand it, and I said so.

I'd heard that dads treat their kids the way their own dads treated them, so I asked Beau, "Is your dad like you, real patient and stuff?" But Beau just laughed.

Eventually, Claude became such a drag that even Beau admitted it was time to go home. Just as we got back, my dad appeared—with Cora. "Hi, guys," Dad called. He was carrying two big bags.

Beau and I said hello.

"We brought Chinese, Big Guy," Dad said, handing me a bag to hold while he got out his key.

Then Cora put her hand on my shoulder and said, "I'm so sorry about your dog, John." Dad had his back to me, unlocking the door. Beau shuffled his feet.

So, I thought, Dad *did* know about Ditz. He'd just been too chicken to tell me himself. And *now* he was too chicken to face me alone. I shoved the bag into Cora's hands and stooped for a fistful of gravel to hurl off the balcony. I threw it as hard as I could. Cora followed Dad inside.

"So you gotta go now?" Beau asked.

I shrugged. I didn't want to go in there.

"Guess me and Claude'll go tell His Ugliness that you know Carter." Beau snickered. "He'll croak!"

Claude giggled. "Uggiess oak!"

It seemed the food had gotten cold on the way home, so Cora was in the kitchen heating it up. Dad had the TV on, of course. Over its babble, he said, "Sorry I lost my temper back there, Big Guy. It was a rough day."

His was a rough day?

I went into the guest room and called home. Liz told me they had decided to have Ditz cremated and to spread her ashes around the backyard. "Do you want us to wait till you get home? Have a memorial service together?"

"I don't know," I said.

"You want to think about it a while?"

How would I think about *that?* "I never should've left her," I said.

"Left Ditz?" Liz asked.

I grunted.

"You blaming yourself?" she asked.

I grunted again.

"Well, don't. You wanna blame someone, blame me. I was there."

She didn't get it.

"Listen," Liz whispered, so I figured Mom had come into the room. "Forget guilt. Grief is bad enough." Then in her regular voice she said, "Here's Mom."

"I miss you," was my mother's hello. "Isn't it time to come home yet?"

"Almost," I said.

"Have you been okay?" That was her worried-about-my-asthma voice.

I heard Liz in the background say, "*Mom!* Give the kid a break!" Then she grabbed the phone back and asked, "How's the Phantom?"

I laughed. "Same."

"Maybe he can't help it," Liz said. "I've been thinking about it. Maybe he *wants* to be a good father but he's just entirely clueless. That's what Jet thinks, anyway."

"Dad didn't tell me about Ditz," I whispered. "He knew but he didn't say anything."

Liz sighed. "Maybe he couldn't think what to say. I know that sounds totally lame—no one *ever* knows what to say, and they just go ahead and say something anyway. But still, maybe Dad's just, I don't know, scared of you. Of us. Of doing the wrong thing. Of being a crummy father."

"Huh?"

Then Liz said, "*Ooops!* Jet's here!" and I heard the clunk of the receiver being dropped on the kitchen counter. I pictured Jet. He was so tall, he practically had to bend his shaved head to walk through our door.

"Johnny?" It was Mom again. "Sweetheart? Are you all right?" This was her worried-about-my-happiness voice. She had a range of worry tones.

"I'm fine, Mom," I said, missing everything about home, but letting my voice sound more annoyed than I felt.

We sat around the table and ate the Chinese food with the TV on. I was thinking about Liz, wondering if she felt bad for not coming to California. At least that would explain why she'd said all that junk about Dad wanting to be a good father but not knowing how, or whatever.

Meanwhile Cora was going on and on about a cat she'd had that died. I didn't listen too closely.

Then Dad said a guy he'd seen that day believed that dogs are reincarnated into good solid trucks. Dad laughed, saying the guy was convinced that his Mitsubishi had the soul of his old boxer, Bub.

So he'd talked about my dog to everyone but me. He knew Bub's name, but I bet he didn't know Ditz's. Liz was way off base thinking Dad couldn't help being a lousy father. In fact, he was a perfect lesson in exactly how *not* to be a father. Never mind *father,* how about just human being? Wouldn't a normal person say *something* nice to a kid whose dog had just died? Not Dad—he *laughs* about dead dogs. Ha, ha, ha.

And what would *you* be reincarnated as, I wanted to ask him. A puny, overpriced, yellow convertible?

After dinner, Cora did the dishes while my father paced back and forth, talking on the phone. I grabbed a book off the bookshelf and took it back to the guest room. Day two.

chapter seven

In the morning, Dad banged on my door and yelled, "Hustle, Big Guy! We've got a meeting at nine."

"We?" I mumbled, stumbling out of bed.

Dad must've already run and showered. He was fixing my eggs, wearing nothing but boxer shorts. His back was hairy. I wouldn't mind some body hair—a huge mustache would be fine—but I could do without the hairy back. It probably won't happen anyway. I take after my mom's side. Straight brown hair, not curly black like Dad's.

He plunked my plate down in front of me and whistled off to his room to dress. The eggs looked gloppy, and the idea of slogging through a plate of them every morning made me wish Ditz were there. I'd just slip my plate under the table and the eggs would be gone in one slurp.

Then I remembered about Ditz. My fork froze halfway to

my mouth. It still wasn't real. It was like a sad movie or book I had read long ago.

I ate. Then I dressed.

Dad came out and looked at me. Something flashed across his face—annoyance? Disappointment? Maybe I imagined it. But then he said, "Got anything a little nicer than that?" So I went back and changed from my T-shirt to a button-down. That was the best I could do.

Beau was just coming out of his apartment as we passed it. "Where to?" he asked, falling in step with us. "The diner?"

"Work," Dad said. "I have a presentation to give."

"Harsh!" Beau said. "Work on such a beautiful morning!" And he waved as we ducked down the stairwell.

Beautiful? The sky was yellowish and the sun was already going full blast, practically sucking the spit out of my mouth. I almost wished I were staying at the apartment to swim. But maybe going to work with Dad would be okay this time. After all, I'd come to California to see *him*.

When we drove out of the parking structure, we zipped along in our little yellow convertible, then pulled into another underground parking garage. We had to wind deeper and deeper to find a spot to bury the car.

"What happens to these things in earthquakes?" I asked, eyeing the massive concrete pillars and imagining us squashed like a yellow bug.

"We don't have time to find out," Dad said with a laugh. "I'm already four minutes late. And Bill Frederick is not a man who appreciates lateness."

Dad hopped out of the car and rushed toward the exit sign. I hurried after him, up some stairs, more stairs, more, then through a door, and into a lobby—without ever having stepped outside.

Dad pointed to a chair. "I'll be down in about . . ." He looked at his watch. "I don't know. As soon as I can." Then he hurried to the elevator, and let it swallow him whole.

I sat on the chair. Men and women tromped in wearing suits, carrying briefcases, not noticing me. I looked around, counted things: doors, squares of marble in the floor, plants. I didn't even have a book or my watch or *anything* to do.

I wondered if Beau's brother was beating him up back at the apartment, which then reminded me of Alex. I hadn't thought of Alex in ages. He was this fifth-grade jerk who bullied me on the bus all through third grade. I don't know what happened to him; he only went to my school that one horrible year, then disappeared—to destroy some other kid's life in some other school, I guess.

I remembered the stomachache I got every day at the bus stop. Those rides were misery. Alex grabbing my books and not giving them back, tearing them or dropping them in the mud. Snatching away my homework and reading it out loud to anyone who'd listen. Calling me "Worm."

My skin crept. All these years later, I still hated him. But maybe it's different if your tormentor is your own brother. Maybe Eric was okay sometimes. Maybe he and Beau had some sort of pact.

My friend Theo back home fought with his little brother,

Jeremy. Theo called Jeremy names and chased him away when he hung around us too long. But Theo didn't *hate* Jeremy. He didn't *hit* him. Well, a shove once in a while, when Jeremy was out of control, but nothing terrible.

Wait, it didn't seem terrible to *me*, but maybe it did to Jeremy. I didn't like thinking my buddy Theo was as big a jerk as Eric, though, so I shook all of them out of my head. I concentrated on closing one eye at a time to make the plant in the corner jump back and forth. I wished I'd brought a book or my Game Boy or Walkman or *something*.

About nineteen hours later I went over to look at the building directory. There were DDS's (that's dentists), and some GP's and an ob-gyn (all doctors). And two CPA's (accountants), and lots of JD's (lawyers). But there were a bunch of other names with initials after them that I didn't know how to decode.

I looked for Bill Frederick. The only Frederick was a Louis and Frederick Enterprises Inc., A.I.A. in suite 7392. What could A.I.A. be, I wondered. American Igloo Advocates? American Independent Armies? How about Aggravating Industrial Ailments like Annoying Itchy Armpits?

I went back to my chair. I tried holding my breath to the count of one hundred. I made faces at my reflection in the glass door. Then I had to pee. Then I *really* had to.

I squirmed around in my chair for a while until it was unbearable. Then I went in search of the men's room. A woman appeared but I couldn't ask *her*. And anyway, she walked right past and didn't even *see* me.

Maybe I'd become invisible, in which case I could just

pee right here in the lobby! There was no one around, but even if there were, all they'd see would be a yellow stream coming out of nowhere. Or maybe my pee was invisible too. I turned down a hall and there was the men's room, but it was locked!

It was getting *really* serious now. I hurried to the elevator and pushed the button eighty times until the door opened. Suite 7392 would be where? The seven thousandth floor? The seventy-third? I poked seven. The elevator dragged s-l-o-w-l-y upward; the doors s-l-o-w-l-y opened far enough for me to squeeze through. I bolted down the hall, looking for the Bill Frederick who did not appreciate lateness.

There! Big glass doors, gold letters. I shoved the door open onto the largest, fanciest office I'd ever seen outside of the movies. A receptionist behind a very shiny desk looked surprised to see me.

Somehow I got it across that my dad was in that office somewhere and that I needed the bathroom. By then I felt about one and a half seconds from taking a giant leak on the Oriental rug.

The receptionist obviously didn't believe me. Probably boys who didn't *really* have dads there rode the elevator up to try to con her all the time. Maybe guarding the executive washroom from intruders was a significant part of her job. Finally, she pushed a button and spoke carefully through her intercom. "Excuse me, sir. But there's a little boy here who *says* his father is inside."

She turned back to me. "What's your name, honey?" she asked with what Liz calls "artificial sweetener."

"John," I barked, about to burst.

"He *says* his name is John and he'd like to use the bath-room."

Did I hear a *laugh* come from that intercom? At least it was followed by a "Sure."

So the receptionist got up s-l-o-w-l-y from her fat leather chair, walked s-l-o-w-l-y over to another huge door, and opened it onto a room that looked more like a living room than an office. Then she *finally* said, "Second door on the right."

I ran.

It wasn't until I was finished that it occurred to me to be embarrassed. Now I had to go back out there and thank the receptionist and have her know I had just peed.

That done, I slunk down to the lobby to count plants again. I had no idea if I'd been there four hours or four years.

When Dad finally stepped off the elevator, I practically lunged at him, like Ditz does when I come home. Like Ditz *did*, not *does*, I reminded myself. That slowed me down, and it's a good thing, because Dad was with another man and it would've looked very undignified if I'd hurled myself at them with my tongue hanging out all slobbery and my tail wagging.

The other guy said, "So this must be your son." He was grinning broadly, probably thinking, The son who pees.

Dad introduced us. It wasn't Frederick, it was some other mister. He and my dad stood around yakking for a while. I was afraid one of them was about to ask the other if he'd like to get some lunch, and the other would say, "Sure!"

I straggled after them, down through the parking pit. But eventually, they shook hands and Dad led me toward his Porsche. The other guy got in a huge black Benz.

I waited for Dad to say something about my coming up to Louis and Frederick Enterprises Inc. But he didn't, so I didn't either. Instead, I asked what A.I.A. stood for and he said it was an architectural firm.

Then he told me his presentation had gone longer than anticipated, so now he had to get to his next appointment and there wasn't time for lunch. *Grrrrrrr!* went my stomach,

Same thing—underground parking garage, down, down. Then rush up another metal-and-concrete stairwell, and hurry into a lobby. I bet it was possible in Los Angeles to live in one place and work in another and not have any idea what either building looked like from the outside.

Dad wasn't out of breath, but I was. I patted my pocket to make sure my inhaler was still there.

"Do you have to use the toilet?" Dad asked me. Sheesh. Was he gonna ask me that all the time now?

"No," I said, and Dad sprinted through a door, calling, "Catch ya in a bit."

"Define *bit!*" I wanted to shout out after him. But he was gone.

This lobby had a little shop in it, at least, so I went in and bought myself a Milky Way, wishing I had more money on me. I poked around and looked at magazines until I got tired of the way the guy behind the counter eyed me like I was going to steal something.

I went back out to the lobby and slumped in a chair,

feeling sorry for myself. Very, very sorry for myself. Bored, lonely, mad. Why had I thought going to work with Dad meant he'd be with me? That he'd pay attention to me. I was so stupid!

If I had any idea where I was, maybe I'd have grabbed a bus and gone back to swim with Beau. Or what if I just walked out the door and disappeared for a while? I'd like to see my dad try to explain *that* to Mom! Ha!

Or why not just get myself to the airport and fly home? Not warn anyone. Just turn up.

I thought of my friends Theo and Brad. Wouldn't they be surprised to see me back early? They said a week in California sounded so great. But they didn't imagine me left to rot in the lobby of one stupid office building after another. Leaving me is what Dad does best, I thought. He's been doing it one way or another my whole life.

chapter eight

There was a clock on the wall, so I knew it took forty-seven minutes for my dad to reappear. This time I didn't want to run up to him; I wanted to *kick* him!

"Sorry, Big Guy," he said, not sounding nearly sorry enough. "Hungry?"

Yes yes yes yes yes! I thought, but all I did was sorta shrug and kinda nod.

"We could pick up a bag of burgers and take it back to the pool," Dad said.

I did another shrug and nod. "Whatever."

He didn't seem to notice the black clouds of fury billowing out of my ears. He just sang along with the oldies on the radio as he drove. Dinosaur rock wasn't as bad as the garbage Cora listened to, but still. I looked over at him, singing, hair blowing. He's a happy man, I thought. And that made me even sulkier.

I saw Beau before he saw us. He had his little brother Claude on his hip and was leaning over the railing, pointing things out to him. Claude had pants on this time. When he saw us, Beau galloped up, making Claude's head bob like a balloon. I was glad to see them, and glad that they followed us home.

Beau and Claude eyed our food until Dad gave them some. Luckily, we'd bought tons. When we were finished, Dad suggested that Beau and I go for a swim. He said he had paperwork to do. Reports to write up. Obviously, I'd been dismissed.

I put on my trunks.

Beau leaped around in the water with Claude hanging on his neck like a baby chimp. Claude squealed and shrieked, not at all bothered by water in his nose, mouth, eyes. He was a brave and *very* noisy little guy, making it almost impossible to talk. But between Claude's outbursts, Beau asked me if I'd had fun with my dad.

"No," I said.

"None?"

"None. He left me sitting around having to pee all day."

"Harsh," Beau said, shaking his head sympathetically.

"Arsh!" Claude copied.

I asked Beau what his dad did.

"Paints," Beau said.

"Houses?" I asked.

"Murals. For banks and stuff, sometimes on the walls of freeways. Ever see the one on the four-oh-five? Dancers?"

I didn't know the 405 from the 134, but we *had* whisked by a huge mural of dancers with wild costumes. My mouth popped open. "Your dad painted that?" I asked. "For real?"

Beau nodded as if it were no big deal. Claude threw his head back, dipping into the water, and Beau spun him around.

"Your *dad?*" I asked again. "He painted that giant thing on the freeway?"

Beau nodded again and looked surprised that I was so impressed. "Yeah, that's what he does."

"Wow!" I said. "That's *amazing!*" I tried to imagine having a dad like that instead of one who scurries underground between office buildings. *"Wow!"* I said again.

Beau smiled in a puzzled way, as if he didn't get what I was so excited about. He and Claude kept playing.

"Mine sells computer support systems, ya know," I explained.

"And that's bad?" Beau asked.

"Well, not *bad,*" I said. "Actually, who knows if it's bad? I'm not even sure what the heck it *means.* But painting gigantic murals on freeways—now, *that's* the coolest thing I've ever heard of in my *life!*"

I added, "I'd like to meet your dad. I've never met a real artist."

"Well, maybe you'll meet him sometime," Beau said. "But probably not. He's not around all that much." Then he let loose a brilliant belch—loud and long. I can almost never get one out like that.

My dad came out of his apartment and leaned over the

balcony. "Hey, Big Guy," he called down, "time to get dressed for dinner."

"What's the plan?" I asked.

"Cora's picking us up in half an hour," he answered.

I guess I made a face, because Beau said, "At least he takes you with him."

"Yeah, terrific," I scoffed.

Beau shrugged and bounced Claude, making huge waves.

I dragged myself slowly out of the pool, up the stairs, and into the apartment. Maybe my slowness or my silence tipped Dad off to my lack of enthusiasm, because he said, "Cora was trying to be nice last night, ya know—telling you about her cat."

I didn't answer.

"You could have been a little more receptive. Polite at least," Dad said.

"I didn't do anything rude," I blurted. "It's not like I told her to shut up." I felt my voice raise to a yell. "I didn't even tell her to mind her own business and *leave me alone!*"

Dad's mouth opened and closed like a trout. Meanness surged through my body. I felt it in my arms and fingertips. It felt *great,* so I added, "I didn't say a word about her weird eyebrows, or her stupid gum chewing, or the fact that she owes me two dollars, or even that she's *always here!* In fact, I think I've shown *incredible* self-control!"

Dad didn't move. I glared at him for a second, then darted into the guest room and slammed the door behind me. I'd never yelled at Dad before. Mom, sure, all the time, but Dad? *Never.*

My heart was pounding. I stood just inside the door, listening. No sound out there except the television. Maybe I'd shocked him into a heart attack and he'd keeled over dead. No, I would've heard him hit the floor.

After a bit, I realized I was shivering in my damp suit. I started dressing, still listening as hard as I could and hearing nothing.

What would he do? Scenes raced through my head. Dad, apologetic, saying, "Gee, I'm sorry, John. If I'd known you didn't like Cora, I never would've let her through the door!" Or him begging, "Let me make it up to you, son! Just name it." Dad furious: "How dare you insult the woman I love? Get out of my house and never come back!"

Or would he give me the silent treatment? Maybe he'd keep me here the rest of the week but not say a word to me.

Minutes and minutes passed.

Then I heard one knock on my door. "I trust you'll show more common courtesy tonight," he said in no particular voice—not barking, not apologetic, obviously not ignoring me. A calm voice, as if I weren't worth reacting to. As if nothing of importance had just happened.

"Don't count on it," I muttered. But I'm sure he didn't hear me, because the buzzer sounded just then and I heard Cora's voice.

He *is* Dr. Ray from Outer Space, I thought. He *looks* human but has no real feelings. No human reactions. A chill ran down my neck as I realized I'd *always* be a stranger in Dadland.

I took my time. When I came out, they were both all

smiles. Dinner was still a go. Cora drove, Muzak playing. We went to a Korean restaurant. Cora acted like it was the biggest deal. As if there were no such thing as Korean food in Kansas. I told her we ate it all the time back home.

First the waiter brought little bowls of stuff for us to share. One looked exactly like slugs. Another was a gob of weeds like something Ditz would hork up after eating grass in the yard. I tasted the one that looked the least weird, and it was so spicy, I knew my mouth was ruined for life. *After* I had a wad of it burning in my mouth, Cora casually said, "That kimchi's a little hot."

I could imagine her taking me for a walk through a mine-field and not mentioning the land mines till my leg was blown off. But I did *not* give her, or my father, the satisfaction of watching me spit it out. I swallowed, I lived. From then on, I stuck to the beef.

They talked. I aged. I could *feel* myself growing old, wrinkled, withered, bald, dried out, stooped over.

If I'd been sure it would hurt their feelings, and not just make them laugh, I would've clicked my heels together and said, "There's no place like home! There's no place like home!"

Then I realized that even *home* wasn't going to be any-place like home from now on, with no Ditz.

After the Korean restaurant we stopped for ice cream. I could tell they thought it would be a huge treat for me, so I didn't order any. I wasn't rude, just said, "No, thank you. I detest ice cream." Then I folded my arms and tried to ig-nore the sight of Cora and my father feeding each other tastes of their cones. It was all I could do to keep from puking.

When we *all* got back to the apartment, Cora said, "Somebody looks mighty sleepy"—meaning me. Sheesh! As if I needed a *hint* that I wasn't wanted, that I was in the way. As if I'd been planning to curl up with them on the couch!

I slunk off to the guest room without a word.

chapter nine

When I woke up the next morning, I thought about Ditz. It was like pressing a bruise to see if it still hurt. I imagined her coming into my room at home to sniff me awake with her wet nose. But still my tears didn't come, which made me feel proud but kind of broken too. Wasn't there something *wrong* with a person who didn't cry about things like this? Maybe it was macho, but it was also sort of . . . what? Disrespectful?

Cora was there, in the living room. I couldn't tell—and didn't want to know—whether she spent the night or left and came back. Cora said my dad was out running. She also told me that they thought it might be fun to go to the beach. "Does that sound good to you, John?" she asked.

I mumbled, "I guess."

"We're going to pick up my niece Iris on the way. You met her."

That meant the plan was already set, so it wouldn't have

mattered if I'd said, "I guess," or, "I'd rather be eaten by warthogs." But I *did* want to go to the beach. Plus, Iris was funny and now I'd get to see her in a bathing suit. I went back to my room—I mean the *guest* room—to get ready.

Iris was waiting in front of her house, wearing a huge hat. I mean *huge!* And a T-shirt that would have been big on a sumo wrestler. Didn't she care what people at the beach would think?

As soon as she got in beside me, she said, "I heard about Toto. That's so sad!"

How was I supposed to answer that? "Thank you"? Or "Oh, that's okay"? Or what? I shrugged—which felt stupid too. But Iris didn't seem to notice; she was still talking. "My mom says it probably won't seem very real to you until you go home and he's not there."

"*She,* not *he.* Ditz is a girl . . . was a girl," I said lamely. Then I looked out the window. I saw a man walking a dog that looked nothing like Ditz, but still.

Beau had been right: It was a long way to the beach.

Cora's trunk was full of stuff that we had to haul across the hot sand: coolers, umbrellas, chairs, blankets, towels, bags. When Cora unpacked a camera, I hoped she'd take a picture of me with Iris and give me a copy that I could take home to show Brad and Theo.

It wasn't that Iris was so incredibly beautiful or anything, but she *was* a girl and she didn't go to our school, which counted for a lot. Plus, she was a *California* girl.

Cora pulled a radio out of her bag and I winced. I like music, all kinds of music—except the spit Cora listens to. Now everyone on the beach would hear her stupid Muzak and see *me* and think *I* liked it!

Click. Radio on. *Glack!* I wished I had earplugs. I thought of grabbing the radio and hurling it into the water, or burying it ten feet in the sand. Better stomp on it first, though, I told myself.

I looked around. Luckily, the beach was pretty empty. A few old people were walking along the edge of the water. There was a family on a blanket, but they were too far away to hear Cora's stupid music or notice Iris's hat.

Iris took off her big T-shirt. Underneath she was wearing a baggy black one-piece suit—not the bikini I'd imagined.

No one was putting on sunblock, so I didn't take mine out at first. I didn't want to seem like a sissy. But then I remembered the blistering lobster burn I got last summer. I did *not* want to go through that again.

"Can I have some?" Iris asked. She carefully dabbed sunblock on her legs. "I'm gonna see if I tan with white polka dots," she said. "An experiment!"

Then she and I left my dad and Cora, and went down to the water. "I think they make a cute couple, don't you?" Iris asked me.

I wondered if I should tell her that my dad had a different girlfriend every summer. I just shrugged again instead.

We dove in and out of the waves. I'd forgotten how strong the ocean is. One wave knocked me over and tossed me around until I didn't know which way was up. I was just starting to panic when I was suddenly s-c-r-a-p-e-d along the sand and thrown up on the shore. My eyes, nose, ears, and mouth were packed with sand. I spit out a mouthful—*yecch!*

There was Iris, just as ground-up and gritty as me, but she was laughing. She started digging near the water's edge, and I went over to help. We worked together for a while and built what I thought was a pretty great sand castle. Iris said it looked like Oz, but it didn't.

When we were finished, I jumped on it. Iris screamed, *"What are you doing?"*

I stopped jumping and said, "Huh?" I had no idea what she was mad about.

"What'd you go and do *that* for?" she yelled, red in the face. "You ruined it!"

"That's the point of building it," I said. "Right?"

"Wrong!" she huffed. "I can't *believe* you did that!" And she stomped into the water.

There was still a tower standing and my feet were itching to kick it down, so I did, but not with much enthusiasm. What was wrong with her? The tide was going to wreck it later anyway.

Then Iris came charging toward me. I just stood there like a dolt until she got right up to me and spit a huge mouthful of water in my face! Then she shrieked away and I chased her into the waves. We splashed each other as hard as we could until we were freezing and had to run back to our towels.

I lay there next to Dad, feeling the sun dry my skin in little itches and snacking on the food Cora had brought. Her stupid radio completely drowned out the sound of the surf, but the food was okay and there was a lot of it. Seagulls came from everywhere.

When Iris and I headed back down to the water, she said, "What do you think happened?"

"Huh?" I asked.

"Between your father and my aunt."

"Huh?" I repeated intelligently.

"They must've gotten in a fight! Didn't you notice that they're not *speaking* to each other?"

How *could* they speak over the blare of that idiotic radio? I wanted to ask. But instead I made my usual response: I shrugged.

"Come on! You mean you didn't notice all that 'Please pass the/no thank you' stuff? That's how grown-ups fight! That's *exactly* how my parents fight. Very polite, *intensely* phony."

I shrugged again.

Iris rolled her eyes in exasperation and huffed, *"Men!"* Then she flounced off into the water.

Men? Me? *Cool!*

A minute later Iris seemed to have forgiven me for being a *man* and we dove into the waves some more. I, for one, didn't go as far out this time, though. I did not want to repeat the sand-eating thing.

When we went back to the blanket, I made a point of noticing Dad and Cora. Iris was right; they were *very* quiet. Then Cora said it was time to leave. Already? She hadn't taken a single picture of me and Iris. Cora and Dad hadn't even gone near the water, but I remembered Beau saying that Dad didn't swim.

It was very quiet in the front seat all the way home—except for Cora's breathing. She was doing a lot of huffing and sighing. Iris and I played twenty questions and ours were the only voices. I snuck peeks at her. It didn't look like the polka-dot experiment had worked. Iris's leg touched mine twice. I wondered if she noticed.

Cora dropped me and Dad off first. She just pulled up in front of Dad's building and we got out. Iris and I said, "Bye," but Dad just grunted and Cora silently stared straight ahead. Good, I thought. No more Cora was just *fine* with me—although I wouldn't have minded seeing Iris again.

When we got upstairs, Beau came galloping up as if he'd been waiting all day, like Ditz. He was dragging Claude along by the hand. Beau took one look at us and said, "The *beach?* Without *me?* Harsh!"

Both Dad and I laughed. "I'm gonna hop in the shower," Dad said. "Then I've got a ton of work to do. Why don't you guys . . ." He made a get-lost gesture with his hand.

I was caked with sand and itchy with salt. "Well, I need to shower too," I said, hearing the whine in my voice. I wanted to pull out my tongue.

Dad just nodded at his whimpering son. "You go first," he said.

I ducked into the apartment and took the fastest shower in the history of bathing.

chapter ten

Beau got rid of his little brother, and we headed for the Laundromat where he said there were video games. As we walked, kicking things down the street, we told corny dumb-blonde jokes, making up our own. Then I told him that my dad and Cora had gotten into a really quiet fight. "So quiet that Iris had to tell me about it."

"Who's Iris?" Beau asked.

"You don't know Cora's niece?" I said.

Beau shook his head, so I guess he didn't know *everything* about my dad.

Then, out of nowhere, Ditz was on my mind. It kept happening, like terrorist attacks—grief ambush with no warning. But there was still something numb about it. I wondered if the numbness was because I was here instead of there. Could distance make death seem less real? Did that mean that if my dad dies while I'm back home in Kansas, *his* death will seem unreal too?

I suddenly felt stupid for thinking these things. Did other guys, guys like Beau, ever think about their parents dying and junk like that? Maybe I was just weird.

"You dreaming about her?" Beau asked, poking me with his elbow.

"Huh?"

"The niece," Beau snickered. "You zoned right out."

"I was, uh, thinking about something else," I stammered.

"Sure you were," Beau kidded, jabbing me in the ribs again.

I tried to remember what we were talking about. "Did you ever see people fight quietly?" I asked him.

"My parents are screamers," Beau said. "Door-slamming screamers." By that time we were at the Laundromat playing games. Beau went through way more quarters than me.

When we were both out of money, we went back to the apartment building and threw rocks from the back steps near the trash cans. Then Beau's brother Eric appeared. I practically ducked, half expecting to get clocked on the head.

"Got any dough?" Eric asked.

Beau shook his head.

Eric pointed at Beau as if his finger were a gun and said, "Deliver."

Beau turned his pockets inside out as proof of poverty. I just stood there, afraid Eric was going to ask *me* for money. But he never looked at me or gave any sign that he'd noticed

I was there. Then he turned and sauntered away, calm, in control.

I exhaled and that kid Alex from back home popped into my head. Alex had been calm like that too. It never seemed particularly thrilling to him that he was ruining my life. Like Eric, Alex tortured in an offhand way as if he were just killing time. Meanwhile, I'd be cowering, feeling my chest close up, trying not to cry, wishing I were dead.

Back then I'd thought that if I had a dad, a *real* live-in dad, I'd ask *him* what to do about it. But it wasn't a long-distance phone call kind of problem. Plus, I'd been afraid Dad would agree with Alex that I was a worm, for having to ask him what to do.

I hadn't told Mom because I knew she'd get hysterical, run to the principal, and make a scene. And I hadn't told my sister because she would've said to go for Alex's jugular. And if Liz had found out that I couldn't fight back, she would've come to my school and beaten Alex to a pulp *for* me.

Having my enemy beaten up by my sister would've been fatally uncool. Having him annihilated by my big *brother,* however, would've been fine. In fact, all my fantasies of re-venge back then included a brother the size of an oak tree who'd obliterate Alex, growling, "This is for John. And *this* is for John," with every bone-crushing blow.

But how did it work, I wondered, if your enemy *was* your big brother? I watched Beau continue to pitch stones at the garbage can as if nothing had happened. One of his pockets was still sticking its tongue out.

"You're lucky you have a sister," Beau said. I thought he meant *instead of a brother who tortures you,* until he added, "You probably understand girls, know how to talk to them and stuff."

"Sisters aren't *girls!*" I said, and we both cracked up.

"Those girls at the corner the other day," Beau said. "They liked you, I could tell."

"Me?" I wished he was right, but was sure he wasn't. "You're crazy. If they were looking at me at all, it was because they'd never seen anyone walk into a cactus before!"

Beau rolled his eyes, as if I were nuts.

I pointed after Eric. "So, did you tell him about Chet Carter?"

"I've been saving it," Beau said. "It's too good to waste."

Then his mom called him in to dinner and I went back to Dad's. The TV was on. Dad was working at the computer and talking business on the phone at the same time. He nodded at me, but that was it. Even while I'm here, I thought, I don't make much of an impression on him. I went to the guest room and picked up the mystery novel I'd started the night before. But after a while, Dad came to the door and said, "Phone for you, Big Guy."

Oh, no! I thought. Mom with more bad news? But it wasn't my mom; it was Iris. I hoped my voice wouldn't squeak.

"How's your father?" she asked me.

"Dad?" I said. "He's fine."

"What do you mean, *fine?*"

"What do you mean, what do I mean?" I asked.

"Well, my aunt is a total *wreck!*" Iris said. "She was crying so hard it was *scaring* me. Driving back here from your house I thought she was going to kill us both! I'm *sure* she couldn't see the road."

"What's the matter with her?" I asked.

"What do you *mean,* what's the matter?" Iris shrieked. "Didn't your dad say *anything?* Isn't he at least acting sad?"

I peeked around the door. Dad was clicking away at his computer. He looked like he always looks. "Maybe he seems a little down," I lied. "I dunno."

"Well, *talk* to him!" Iris said. "Maybe we can fix this! I can't stand seeing Auntie Cora so miserable. And I was really counting on being a bridesmaid."

"What am I supposed to say?"

"I don't know. He's *your* father. Think of something! I'll call you later." And Iris hung up.

I peeked back out at Dad. I wondered if his fight had anything to do with the stuff I'd said about Cora. For a second it felt *great* to think he'd broken up with Cora just because I hated her. It felt great and it felt *right*—that's what parents should do for their kids!

Great and right, maybe—but not very likely. Dad didn't exactly have a history of doing stuff just to please *me.* But still.

I lay back down and picked up the novel where I'd left off. I was having trouble keeping all the characters straight, and in my opinion, there were way too many descriptions of scenery and whatnot. But I figured that if I just kept my eyes moving across the page, my brain would eventually catch up.

A couple of chapters later, Dad called out, "Who's hungry?"

"Me!" I called back.

"Let's get some chow!" Dad said.

My first thought was, Just us? Me and him? Thank goodness he'd broken up with Cora, or for sure she'd be tagging along!

I knew Iris would want me to grill my father on the Cora business, but I wasn't about to blow this. In the car, he told me that he was having a great year at work. He said that he *loved* his job and that he hoped one day I'd find something that satisfied me in the same way.

I almost asked him if he thought sales would be right for *me* too. But how would *he* know? Anyway, I wasn't a hundred percent sure exactly what it was that Dad sold, and it would have sounded incredibly stupid to ask him *now*, to admit that all this time I haven't had any idea what he does for a living. Instead, while he talked, I listened for clues.

I'd asked Liz once what it meant to sell computer support systems and she'd said Dad sold cyber-bras and jockstraps for computers. "Get it?" she'd asked. "*Support*? Bras?" I hadn't gotten it at the time, but I did later and was totally embarrassed.

If Dad ran out of steam talking about work, I planned to bring up Liz's boyfriend. Jet would be good for a few laughs, with his shaved head and everything.

But we got to the restaurant before Dad was finished talking about his work. It was a seafood place and it smelled like it. We got a table and were just looking at the menu, when a man and woman suddenly appeared and said, "Matt! What are you doing here? Haven't seen you in, well, way too long!"

Handshakes, kisses, introductions, and then, of course, two chairs being dragged over to our table. Sure, they'd be *delighted* to join us!

I slumped down and kicked the leg of the table. Kick. Kick, kick, kick—until my father said, "Hey, Big Guy, cut that out."

I was three. I was Claude. I was having a tantrum, a sulk. Did I care if my father was ashamed of me? *No!* I gave the table leg another kick.

First they had drinks and that took years. Then they had to discuss the menu *forever.* A typical adventure in Dadland, I thought. But this time I had to admit it wasn't Cora's fault. Maybe it had never been Cora's fault. Or Bobbie's, or . . . who was it the year before? I searched my memory until Nadine appeared. Liz and I secretly called her Sardine.

Those women weren't hogging Dad's time, I realized, or keeping Dad away from us. Dadland was ruled by Dad. This was how he wanted it. He didn't change plans just because his kids were in town. No, he did *exactly* what he would've done anyway. To him there was nothing special about this week, and I would always be a stranger here.

Liz was right. Dad didn't make room for us. I suddenly wished she were here in this stinking seafood restaurant with me. She'd have made it less awful.

At first I'd been scared to go to California without her. But then I got used to the idea, and after a while I was really looking forward to it, imagining all kinds of great father-son moments we'd have, just the two of us. Boy, was I *stupid!*

Kick. Kick. And one more big *kick!*

Dad glared at me.

The waiter brought our food but I'd lost my appetite. My father and his friends, however, were ripping the legs off crabs, prying clam shells open, tearing, dismembering, having a great time. Juice dribbled down the other man's chin. It was the most violent meal I'd ever seen. I closed my eyes.

No, I thought, this is definitely not Cora's fault. Then I felt a little sorry about her crying her eyes out. That joke about clowns tasting funny wasn't so bad, and except for her cats and her eyebrows and music and gum chewing, she was no worse than Bobbie or Sardine or the rest of them. No worse, probably, than next summer's girlfriend would be. Cora had at least tried to say something nice about Ditz—that's more than my own father did!

Remembering Ditz made my chest tighten and I felt in my pocket for my inhaler. If I hadn't come on this *stupid, stupid* trip, I probably would've caught her when she bolted out the door. I would have grabbed her collar as I had a thousand times before. I could see my hand sinking into her spongy black fur. I could feel my fist holding tight to her red leather collar. She'd have given a yank, then realizing she was caught, would have instantly forgotten about charging out the door and wiggled around to lick my face instead. No hard feelings.

I went to the bathroom and gave myself two blasts from

my inhaler. That helped. I came back to the table but still couldn't eat my food.

The adults didn't notice. They splashed around in their plates, creating a funeral mound of shells in the center of the table while they talked and talked. It sounded like work stuff, mostly. Seems my dad did a project with this guy a while back. So what?

If my dad had been a *mural* painter, dangling from scaffolding into the freeway ditch, then it would make sense that people would want to hear about it. If there were gigantic paintings by him all over town . . . But my father just scurried like an ant in a necktie from meeting to meeting.

I watched him smiling, talking. He definitely did *not* look like a man suffering from a broken heart. I wondered if he'd been this calm when he broke up with Mom and left her and Liz and me. What if I'd run into the street and been hit by a car when he left us? Would he have blamed himself? I was just a baby back then. A puppy. I probably didn't understand why Dad left *me* any better than Ditz understood my leaving *her*.

In the car on the way home, I asked, "Where was Cora tonight?"

Dad shrugged, cool as a rock. "Beats me," he said.

Of course, I probably had Ditz longer than my dad had known Cora. So maybe it wasn't so weird that he wasn't crying. But forget crying—Dad wasn't *anything*-ing. On the other hand, was I showing any signs of having lost Ditz? Did that mean I was like my dad? No no no no no!

✳ ✳ ✳

There's a time difference between California and home and my mom goes to bed early, but I figured I'd call anyway. I didn't wake her; she was up, busily stacking her fears higher and higher as she waited to hear from me.

Once she was convinced that I wasn't dead or dying, Mom said, "I keep thinking I hear Ditz's toenails on the kitchen floor." Then she felt bad for saying that and apologized for making me sadder than I probably already was. She said she hoped that Ditz's death wasn't ruining my trip and that I was having some fun in spite of it all. "Ditz wouldn't want you to be unhappy," Mom choked.

I told her I was having a great time.

When I went back into the living room, Dad told me there was a message from Iris and she'd left me her phone number. He raised his eyebrows at me. I couldn't say the call was about him and Cora, so I let him think Iris liked me. I wondered if that sort of thing impressed him.

But I didn't call Iris back. Three days down. Four to go.

chapter eleven

The phone woke me the next morning. I stumbled into the living room. Dad, in his jogging clothes, was pacing as he talked. He held up the coffeepot, offering me a cup. Of *coffee?* What the heck. I nodded as if I drank it every day.

But then Dad handed me the phone and said, "It's Liz."

"Now who's dead?" I asked her, too groggy to actually panic.

"Jet!" she said. "At least I *wish* he was! Do you know what he said, the creep? You won't *believe* it!"

"Jet?" I asked, tasting my coffee. Awck! Added more sugar, more cream. "Your boyfriend Jet?"

"Oh, *please!* How could I have been so *stupid?*" Liz said. "When I told him about cremating Ditz, do you know what he said?"

"What?"

"He said it was a waste of dog! Said we should take her to a *taxidermist!* Have her stuffed in a mean pose and stick a barking cassette inside her to scare away burglars! He thought that would be *cool!* He thought it was *funny!*"

"It is a *little* funny, Liz," I said.

Dad winked at me. He was smiling. Liz must've told him about it too.

"It is not a bit funny, John! How can you even *say* that?"

"Liz," I tried, "that's why you *liked* Jet! Because you said he doesn't think like everyone else. Shaved head, striped car, all that. He isn't *predictable* and *boring!* Remember?"

Liz's voice went cold. "I thought *you,* of all people, would understand, John."

"Jet liked Ditz," I told Liz. "I'm sure he didn't say that to be *mean.* He was just being . . . *Jet!*"

"Yeah, well, if *that's* who he was being, I hate him."

I sighed.

When I got off the phone, Dad laughed out loud. "That's rich!" he said. "Stuff the family pet!"

I was just about to smile—my face was halfway there— when suddenly it wasn't funny anymore. *The family pet,* as Dad had called her, was *Ditz.*

Jet knew Ditz. He'd taken us to the vet last month when Ditz had hurt her paw and Mom wasn't home. Jet had let her bleed all over the backseat of his striped car. He'd been the one to carry Ditz into the office. Dad hadn't been there. He never even met Ditz.

"Who's this Jet fellow?" Dad asked. "And what's with the *name?*"

I got control of myself. "He's Liz's boyfriend," I said. "At least, he was."

"Did I hear you say he shaves his head? Our Liz is a classy gal," Dad said. "She can do better than a guy like that!"

I was glad Dad thought Liz was classy; I'd have to tell her that. But he didn't know Jet. "He's a nice guy," I said. "I like him. We all do."

Did I see Dad wince when I said *all*? Because the *all* didn't include him?

No, I must've imagined it.

Dad clapped his hands. End of Liz-Jet discussion. *"So,"* he said, "do you just want to stay here today? Swim with Beau?"

I shrugged. "What are *you* going to do?"

"Nothing. It's Sunday."

"You mean you don't have to work?" I asked.

"Nope."

"Not at *all?*"

Dad shook his head. "No."

"No barbecues? Beach plans?"

Dad squinted at me. "Are you trying to tell me something here, Big Guy?"

I shook my head. "It's just . . . you usually have a lot of stuff planned," I stammered.

"Well, we *were* going to go sailing with Cora and some of her friends today," Dad said. "But plans have changed."

That made more sense. Of course Dad hadn't *deliberately* left a day open for me—but still. "You mean we could do something, just *us?*" I asked.

"Sure," Dad said, looking surprised. "Is there something special you wanted to do? You want to go for a drive? Or, I don't know, horseback riding? Or there's a batting cage up on Lexington."

My dad was actually asking me what I wanted to do with him today. Him and me. I'm allergic to horses and I'm not much of a batter. But I didn't want to wreck this. I tried to think fast—what do guys do with their dads? I mean normal guys. Go fishing? Hunting?

"You don't play golf, do you?" Dad asked.

Ack! This was it—the moment when we'd get to know each other, father to son. Man to man. But I couldn't think of a *thing* to tell him about me! What *did* I like to do? My mind was blank. "I'm not too athletic," I confessed, "except for swimming—and Jet taught me to Rollerblade."

Dad lit up. "Rollerblade? No kidding. You any good at it?"

"Not bad," I admitted.

"Think you could teach your old man? There's a place that rents skates down on the pier."

"Sure!" I said. "You bet!"

"Terrific! I've always wanted to try that," Dad said. "I'll just go for my run, take a quick shower, and we'll be off."

"Cool!" I grinned. Then I tried to grin a little less. I didn't want to look like Ditz, wiggling with joy at the mention of a walk. I calmly sipped my horrendous, and now cold, coffee, as if going Rollerblading with my dad was no big thing.

Not two seconds after Dad jogged out the door, Beau showed up. I wanted to shoo him away, afraid Dad would invite him along if he caught sight of him. But I also wanted to brag a bit.

Beau loped in and collapsed in a chair. "Wanna go to the corner, get something to eat?" he asked.

Actually, I was starving, but I wasn't sure how long Dad ran, and if I was late, the whole plan might get screwed up.

"When my dad gets back, we're going Rollerblading," I said. Then I added, "Just *him* and *me*."

"Well, that gives us forty-eight minutes," Beau said, not taking offense.

Beau and his bottomless knowledge of my dad!

"So, whatcha think?" he asked.

"Well, let's hurry, then!" I said, and I wrote Dad a quick note. I put it on the phone because for sure he'd notice it there. But then I froze, wondering if I should leave the door open for him or lock it.

"He's got his key," Beau said.

That was the last straw. "Why do you know so much about my father?" I asked, practically stamping my foot. "You've got your *own* father."

Beau backed away, putting his hands up as if to fend off my punches. "Harsh!" he said. "Harsh words before breakfast!"

I felt like a jerk but I didn't back down. "I *mean* it. I want to know."

Beau scooted past me out the door and said, "Come on, let's eat." Then he pointed to the door next to my dad's apartment. "Two fourteen, Beverly and Lou. Lou has prostate cancer and has to pee into a bag he wears. Beverly works at a spa. She pours hot wax on ladies' legs and armpits, and when it cools, she rips it off, yanking their hair out while they scream."

"You're kidding!" I said.

"For real," Beau insisted. "Ever see signs that say *waxing?* That's what it means!"

"Sheesh! Do you think that's how Cora got rid of her eyebrows?"

Beau shrugged, then nodded toward *his* apartment. "Two twelve, my gene pool."

At the next door he said, "Two ten. Martin Baxter. You seen him?"

I shook my head.

"Nervous guy. He sneaks in and out of his apartment. Acts like he's being followed all the time. He's got three locks on his door. I've been in there to feed his fish, and I've never seen anything worth locking up."

"If he's so nervous, how come he gave you a key?" I asked.

"Not *a* key, *three* keys," Beau said, laughing. "Actually, I have the keys to six apartments here, not counting my own. Including two oh eight. Miss Candy Corn. She used to be a Vegas dancer and has sexy pictures of herself from the old days all over her walls. But that was eons ago. Now she's a skinny old lady, but she still tans her hide at the pool every day from eleven till noon. It's her yippy dog you hear sometimes. When she's too tired to walk him, I do it."

We got to the stairwell, and Beau said, "More?"

I wanted him to tell me about the rest, but I also got his point. "Can you do every apartment in the building?" I asked.

"Except the newlyweds in one oh three. They haven't been here long and they keep to themselves."

"I don't know anything about my neighbors back home," I told Beau, "except which ones have dogs or kids."

"None of these have kids," Beau said. "Me and my brothers, that's it. In fact, this whole area is pretty much an old-fart zone."

"Bummer," I said, and Beau nodded. Then I remembered what we'd been talking about and I asked him how he'd describe the guy in 216.

Beau punched my arm, a little too hard. "Two sixteen? Nice guy. Dates pretty women. Misses his kids. A little shy."

"Shy? He has more friends than anyone! He's got parties and plans all the time . . ."

"I'm no shrink," Beau said. "That's just my impression. The guy can have friends and still be shy, can't he?"

"Well," I mumbled, "compared with you, *everyone's* shy. Who else has the keys to six apartments beside his own?"

We got the same booth at the diner. Beau poured salt on the table again.

I wrestled with my pride for a while, then gave in and asked, "What makes you think he misses his kids?"

"Who? Two sixteen?"

I nodded, trying to look casual.

Beau shrugged. "He brags about them."

Curiosity squelched whatever pride I had left. "*Both* of them?" I asked.

"Sure! He says his daughter is very gutsy and she's in drama, theater, all that. He says she's funny and doesn't take any bull. And he says he has a son who's smart and thoughtful and fair. Says he tries to see both sides of everything and would make a good judge."

"Two sixteen said that?"

"He told me a story about his son getting clobbered by the older sister when he was little. And even while the kid was crying in pain he said, 'She didn't mean to hurt me *this* bad! She was just mad!'"

"He *told* you that?" I said.

Beau rolled his eyes. "Did I make it up?"

I poured some salt on the table and licked it off my finger. "Most kids see their divorced dads every other weekend, dinner on Wednesday, half the summer, Thanksgiving, Christmas vacation . . ." I frowned. "We see him a week a year. Period. And when Liz told him she wasn't coming this time, he didn't even squawk."

"If he'd squawked, would she have come?"

I'd never asked myself that.

chapter twelve

When we got back to our building, Beau stopped at his door and said, "See ya later."

"What're you going to do today?" I asked.

Beau shrugged. "Earn my keep, I guess."

I bet Beau would have liked to go blading with us. But I shook off the thought.

When I got to my dad's apartment, I heard him singing in the shower. The phone was ringing. I answered.

"Well, thanks for calling me back, Tin Man," Iris said sarcastically.

"We were busy," I said. "I didn't have anything to tell you anyway."

"What do you *mean* you didn't have anything to tell me?"

"I mean my dad didn't say anything about your aunt."

"What do you *mean* he didn't say anything?"

I was getting so tired of this that I didn't even try to keep my voice from cracking. "Sorry, Iris," I said. "I gotta go."

"*Men!*" she spat, and hung up.

Dad came out in a towel. "Who was that?" he asked.

"Iris," I admitted.

Dad laughed. "She's really on your trail, isn't she?"

"Actually, Dad, she's on *yours*. She wants to know if you and Cora are going to make up."

Dad raised his eyebrows, stuck a wad of toilet paper in his ear, and dug around in there. "Maybe she's just using that as an excuse to call you," he said. "People drum up all kinds of excuses to call each other. Happens all the time."

I thought about that. Was it possible? "Nah," I said. "She's worried about her aunt."

Dad shrugged. "Cora's a nice lady," he said. "She deserves better than me." Then he smiled. I guess he didn't feel too bad about being undeserving. I didn't say anything. I wasn't exactly rooting for Cora with her *four* cats and her elevator music.

"Beware of the kind of women who like to *help*," Dad said. "At first they just cook for us, sew on buttons. But after a while, they want to pick out our clothes, change our haircuts, correct our speech, our thoughts." Dad shuddered. "It's not entirely their fault, though. I'm convinced it goes way back to the dolls they had as girls."

"Huh?" I said.

"It became clear to me years ago," Dad explained, "when Liz was about six. She held her Ken doll in one hand and hopped him over to her Barbie. Liz made Ken say, 'Hi! You're cute. Want to get married?' And Barbie's answer was, 'Sure! If you wear this!' And she held up a Ken-doll outfit."

I'd have to tell Liz that he remembered that. She might roll her eyes and call Dad a sexist, but still.

Dad got dressed and we headed out. Beau was nowhere to be seen. I was glad in a cowardly way.

"Was Mom one of those women, you know, who wanted to change you?" I asked Dad in the car.

"Your mom? No way! Your mother's a great gal. Really! A very hard act to follow. They don't make many like her."

I chewed on that awhile as we drove. I'd always thought it was Dad's idea to leave us. But I didn't actually remember anyone *telling* me that. Maybe Mom threw him out! Whenever I asked her anything about it, she always gave the same zero-information nonanswer: "Your father and I fell out of love with each other, but we'll both always love you."

My friend Theo's mom told him everything, and I mean *everything*, about why she divorced Theo's dad. And she still, to this day, tells him whenever his dad does anything cruddy, like when he's late sending the child support checks. Theo says I should consider myself lucky that my mom doesn't dump on me. He says a few unknowns are well worth it. But I think it stinks that parents can decide what to tell and what not to, and that's just that.

We got to the pier and rented Rollerblades, knee pads, elbow pads, and helmets, then sat on a bench to put it all on. Dad said he felt like a giant insect. He tried to stand up, but his arms windmilled around, his ankles turned, and he plopped back down on the bench with an explosive laugh.

He grabbed me and hauled himself up, but his feet shot out from under him. I couldn't tell whether he was really as bad at it as he seemed, or he was kidding. *I'd* fallen plenty of times in the beginning—but I was me and Dad was *Dad!*

"This is a blast!" he said. "Why haven't we done stuff like this before?"

I didn't answer.

The other skaters and bikers whizzed past us, some smiling over their shoulders at the spectacle we made. Dad didn't mind. He had his arm around my neck and his butt poking way out in the back.

"Bend your knees!" I instructed, laughing. "Straighten up."

He let go of me and *boom!* Back down on the bench.

We tried again. This time we got about three feet and were on our way, Dad clinging to my neck and giggling like a kid.

After a while he started getting the hang of it, although one of his feet would skid off on its own every now and then, making him clutch at me. By then, I was laughing so hard I could barely breathe. I almost felt like the screaming meemies were on their way.

"*I love this!*" Dad hollered, sounding a little hysterical himself.

We got as far as a hot-dog stand, and Dad said he needed fuel. He bought us each a dog and a Coke. I scarfed mine down but Dad was having trouble. Every time he lifted his drink to his mouth, his feet would slip and he had to fling his arm around to stop himself from falling. I didn't even try not to laugh at him.

Then out of nowhere there was a bicycle, and suddenly the bicycle and my dad were in a heap on the ground, with the biker cursing and my dad saying, "Uh-oh."

Was that ketchup or blood all over the place? I untangled the men and the bike, and helped Dad hobble over to a bench. *Phew!* It was only ketchup. The other guy threw a fit about his busted bike. Dad pulled out his business card and said, "Call me."

The biker snatched Dad's card and grumbled away.

"Too old for this," Dad mumbled, wincing with pain. "Should've listened to the little voice inside my head."

"Where's it hurt?" I asked.

"Everywhere," he said. "Knee."

I helped him take off his knee pad and could practically see his knee getting bigger before my eyes. So what was the *point* of knee pads? I lugged the gear back to the rental place and retrieved our shoes while Dad sat there with Coke in his hair and ketchup all over his shirt. He tried to smile when I got back, but he wasn't very convincing.

"We have to get you to the hospital," I said.

"Can you drive a stick shift?" he asked.

"Me?" I said. "Dad, I'm twelve."

He laughed. "I keep forgetting that! I keep thinking you're just a really short adult."

"Well, the *really short* part is right," I said, trying to put his shoe on for him.

"Yeah? Are you short for your age?" he asked.

"Way short!" I said. "Everyone in my grade is at least a head taller than me. Including the girls!"

"No kidding!" Dad laughed again. "I was the same way! I didn't grow until I was a junior in high school."

I stared at him. "What?"

"Then I grew so fast all at once that my joints were in *agony!* Not like this, though," he said, pointing to his ballooning knee.

It sounds bad that even though my dad was in pain, I was feeling happier than I'd ever been in my whole life. But it's true.

We decided to take a taxi. I'd never flagged one by myself. I walked up to the street but couldn't find any. Not a single cab. I was about to go back down and ask Dad what I should do, but then I saw a phone booth and figured I'd try calling one. I had change in my pocket.

I got the number of a cab company, then checked the name of the street and the address of the tattoo place next to the phone booth. I called and they said they'd be there in ten minutes. Nothing to it.

I went back to Dad, then ran up the street to wait. I was afraid the driver would see I was just a kid and take off, but he didn't. He even helped me get Dad—driver on one side, me on the other, Dad kind of pale and rubbery between us.

The hospital wasn't far, and an orderly met us at the emergency entrance with a wheelchair. There were a ton of insurance forms and whatnot that took forever. Then we had to wait with all the other sick and hurt people, including an enormously pregnant woman who was moaning. Her nervous-looking husband kept telling her to breathe through the pain.

"*You* breathe through it!" she finally barked back at him. And half the people in the waiting room cracked up.

Dad leaned over and whispered to me, "Everyone pretends *both* parents are going to share the birth experience. But once the pain starts, it's a different story."

The pregnant woman was whisked away in a wheelchair with her husband scampering behind. "When your mother was in labor," Dad said, "she wanted a hot pastrami sandwich and a kosher dill in the worst way. But the midwife said she could only have ice chips. Every time I left the room, your mom was sure I was sneaking off to eat. But I swear, I didn't have a single bite the whole time!"

He laughed. "Eventually I got her a KitKat from the vending machine and slipped it to her behind the midwife's back. Your mom was beyond hunger by then, though. All she could do was squeeze it to a pulp, wrapper and all. But I was forgiven." Dad smiled at me. "I think that was the last time I was in a hospital, till now."

I'd never heard that story, or anything like it, before. "Was that my birth or Liz's?"

"Yours," he said.

I'd never pictured Dad at my birth—not that I'd thought about my birth much. But if I had, I would have imagined him pacing in the waiting room on his cell phone. Or handing out cigars to his friends and clients—in California. I'd forgotten that he didn't leave till I was three. I wished I remembered more from back then.

By the time Dad's name was called, his knee was huge and the skin was so tight it looked like it would split. They took X-rays, then we waited around again. But I didn't mind. Throughout the whole ordeal, it was just Dad and me, talking. I figured his talkativeness was the result of shock, but I liked it.

At one point he said, "Stuff like this makes you appreciate what you've got, Big Guy. I'm a lucky man, you know. I love my work. I love my car. I love going out for a run in the morning . . . I've got two legs. I've got you."

When the doctor came in, she talked mostly to me. It reminded me *exactly* of how my doctor back home sometimes ignored me and talked to my mom as if I weren't there. When Dr. Wong did that to *me,* I hated it, but Dad didn't seem to mind.

"We're going to give him a temporary cast, and you'll need to keep him off that leg for two weeks," this doctor told me. "And I mean *off!* Then come back and we'll change this for a walking cast." She turned to my father and talked louder. "Have you been on crutches before, Mr. Gordon?"

"Not for many, many years," Dad said.

"Well, the orderly will be in to give you a refresher course." She wrote out some prescriptions for anti-inflammatories and pain pills and explained to *me* how often Dad should take each one.

Next came the orderly. He wrapped my dad's leg in a cast, then showed him how to use crutches. "You get up to go to the toilet only," the guy said, shaking his finger at Dad. "Understand?"

"Yes, sir," Dad said, like a kid who'd gotten in trouble.

I pushed Dad in a wheelchair to the hospital pharmacy and filled his prescriptions. Then we took a cab home. This cabby, though, was a creep. When I asked him to help me get Dad up the stairs, he said, "Sorry, I've got a bad back," and zoomed away.

I leaned my dad against the wall with his crutches and left him grumbling about the elevator that had been broken for months. I raced upstairs, hoping Beau was home. How would I haul Dad up all those stairs myself? What if I dropped him?

I hammered on Beau's door, and thank goodness he was there. I told him about my dad's accident, and I swear, his eyes pinked up and his face got blotchy, like when I told him about Ditz!

By the time we got Dad upstairs and into a chair, with his cast propped up on the coffee table, Dad looked beat. But he grabbed the phone, saying he had to get his car back, had to cancel appointments for tomorrow, had a million things to do.

Beau and I slipped out of the room. "Major drag," Beau said.

"Actually, we had a great time for a while there," I told him, hearing how stupid that sounded.

Beau asked if I wanted to go feed the hungry video games more quarters, but I said I had to keep an eye on my dad. And it's a good thing I did, because soon he needed help getting to the bathroom. The crutches were clumsy down the narrow hall. They clunked against the wall and

Dad looked like he was going to tip right over. It was funny, and not.

I finally got him back in his chair, and then he said he was hungry.

"Well, we've got eggs and we've got eggs," I said.

Dad smiled. "I think I'll have eggs."

Beau and I banged around in the kitchen, hunting for a bowl and a frying pan. Then Beau pretended he was the host in a cooking show.

"First vee must break zee egg," he said. But when he tapped it against the counter, the egg crunched to a zillion bits, oozing egg slop up his arm.

He came after me with his slimed hand, so I had to sound the battle cry, "Kill Kitchen Creature!" and fire slices of bread at him. Someone knocked over the orange juice and the floor was instantly slippery—and great for sliding.

"Hey! I'm trying to make a call here!" Dad yelled from the living room. Beau and I tried to quiet down—but we couldn't.

Eventually, we brought Dad his food. "Ta-da!" I said. Dad looked at it and tried to hide his wince.

Beau and I flicked through the channels, making fun of the people on TV while Dad talked on the phone and ate every sticky glop of egg and every burnt crumb of toast.

When he hung up, Dad said, "Stuff like this makes you realize how alone you are. What would I have done if you hadn't been here, Big Guy? You too, Beau."

"This wouldn't have *happened* if I hadn't been here," I said. But I knew what he meant.

After a while he fell asleep in his chair. Beau and I tiptoed out to the grocery store.

"Need more eggs," Beau said.

Later, I had to help Dad get undressed and into bed. Now *that* was weird.

After he was settled, I called home. "Mom? I think I've got to stay longer. Dad wrecked his knee. Tore some ligaments."

"What?" she said. "How?"

"I was teaching him to Rollerblade."

"*Rollerblade?*" She laughed. "There's no fool like an old fool. What's that forty-eight-year-old geezer think he's doing on Rollerblades?"

"Mom, he has to stay off his leg completely. I gotta stay."

"Well, you still have a couple of days left," Mom said. "Isn't that enough?"

"He's supposed to stay off it for two *weeks,* not two days."

Mom sighed. "Isn't there someone else who could help him?" she asked.

"No," I said, and heard how lonely and sad that one word was.

chapter thirteen

Dad and I spent the fifth day of my visit playing cards and talking about stuff. He even told me a little about *his* dad, my grandfather I never met. "I hardly knew him," Dad said. "He wasn't mean, exactly, he just couldn't be bothered with me. He was always tired when he came home from work—wanted to be left alone to smoke his pipe and read the paper." Dad shuffled the cards, saying, "My father was old-fashioned. He thought talking to kids was women's work."

I cut the deck and thought, Women's work? And suddenly I just knew that Dad thought that telling me Ditz had been killed was women's work, best left to Mom and even Cora to handle. But somehow that realization made me feel worse for him than for myself.

Dad dealt the cards and said, "I couldn't have friends over when my father was home. My mother was always telling me to be quiet and leave him in peace." I tried to picture Dad as a kid in that kind of gloomy house. "They were older parents," he said. "And, you know, I didn't have brothers or sisters or anything."

I studied my cards, afraid that if I looked right at him, he'd clam up. "I guess I thought my father would become interested in me when I got older," Dad said, taking my jack with his ace. "But that didn't happen. He up and died right before my fifteenth birthday."

Fifteen? I thought. That wasn't all that much older than me.

Dad took a nap after the card game. He said the pain pills made him dopey. I tried to watch TV, but I couldn't stop thinking about Dad and *his* dad.

I was relieved when Beau came over with a tub of vegetarian lasagna from his mother. The three of us devoured it for lunch. I guess Mrs. Lubeck was that *helping* kind of woman who likes to take care of men. She *must* be, I thought, with a husband and four sons! Then I wondered if I was a helping kind of *guy.* The idea creeped me out. But I liked taking care of my dad.

"Your father's a big boy," Mom said on the phone later. "And he has exactly the life he created for himself. I've thought about it, and I want you home as planned, John."

"I can't leave him! He needs me."

"*I* need you," Mom said. "Liz and I need you."

What did *they* need me for? I wondered.

"What am I supposed to tell Theo and Brad?"

"*Mom!* It's just another week," I groaned.

"And we have to figure out what to do with Ditz's ashes. And Liz is crying all the time about Jet."

"Liz is crying?" I asked. That was hard to imagine. "She really broke up with him?"

"She made a bonfire of all his photos and love notes in a pan on the stove. It sent up such a cloud of fumes, we had to stay out of the house all afternoon!"

I smiled. Building a fire sounded more like Liz than crying did. I'd hate to picture my sister all weepy like Cora.

"Plus, John, a new plane ticket home would get expensive," Mom was saying.

"I'll pitch in, out of my savings," I said. "Dad can't even walk to the bathroom himself, Mom. I don't think you get it. He *needs* me!"

"And what about all the times you needed him, Johnny? Where was he then?"

I didn't say anything. I knew she was just missing me. And maybe she was afraid that she'd lose me—that I might choose to make Dadland my home.

"I'm sorry," she finally said. "Do what you think is best, son."

I went into Dad's room. He was watching TV. I admit, I was plenty tired of the constant racket.

"Can I turn this off a second?" I asked.

Dad looked surprised, as if such a thing had never occurred to him. "You bet," he said.

"Dad," I began, "I can stay on longer if you want. I'd be glad to . . . you know, stay on another week or so to help you out."

"That's a mighty nice offer, Big Guy," Dad said. "But it won't be necessary. Really. What kind of summer vacation's that? Hanging around here, watching your old man nod off in his chair?"

"I don't mind," I said.

"You're a good kid," Dad said. "A really excellent kid. But son, I'll be just fine."

"Well, then maybe you should call Cora," I said. "Maybe you two could make up."

"I thought you hated her," he said.

"I don't *hate* her," I insisted. "Her eyebrows are weird, and I don't see why she needs *four* cats, but other than that, she's a nice enough lady. And anyway, she's not *my* girl-friend."

Dad raised his eyebrows.

"You didn't break up with her because of me, did you?" I asked.

"Nah," Dad said with a shrug. "It was just that she sent up a big *warning* flag at the beach. Disaster! Beware!" Dad chuckled. "So, I bewared. Or I beed-ware, whatever."

I thought Dad's pain pills were making him loopy. "Huh?" I said.

"At the *beach!*" he continued. "We were having a per-fectly lovely time. Beautiful day. Sunshine and so on. Then suddenly, Cora said my bathing suit was too ugly to give to the poor. That may not sound like much to *you*, son, but trust me on this one: Them's fighting words! And as if she hadn't gone way too far already, do you know what she said next?"

I shook my head.

"She said to throw it away and she'd buy me a more fashionable one!"

He stared wide-eyed at me, I guess waiting for my gasp of horror. Then he added, "She was probably thinking of one of those minuscule, muscle-man, G-string Speedo things in unspeakable Day-glo colors!" Dad shuddered.

I laughed.

"You know, son," he said, shaking a warning finger, "take it from your old man. It starts with a swimsuit, but the next thing you know, it's lacy curtains in the kitchen!"

"Actually," I said, "you could use something in your kitchen window. Anyone walking by can see you making eggs in your underwear."

Dad squinted at me, scratching his chin where a beard had already started growing.

I squinted back.

Then he sighed as if defeated. "I suppose I could give my old friend Cora a call," he said. "See if she'd like to stop by tomorrow. Maybe bring her niece to say good-bye to you. What the heck."

"What the heck," I agreed.

Dad smiled. "In fact, if you'll excuse me, I think I'll phone her right now. Let her yell at me awhile." He thumped his cast. "I won't be needing a swimsuit in the near future anyway."

I left him alone and put my trunks on, then went outside and knocked on Beau's door. "How about a night swim?" I asked him.

"Cool!" he said, and ducked back in to change.

The pool was lit from underneath, making our bodies look rubbery in the blue-green water. We splashed around, raced. Then we lolled on the steps at the shallow end.

"My dad says I should leave as planned, day after tomorrow," I said.

"You gonna?" Beau asked.

"I guess so. I mean, I can't exactly stay if he doesn't want me to. And my mom wants me home."

"What do *you* want?" Beau asked.

"*Me?*" I said stupidly.

"No, not *you.* I was asking that palm tree," he joked.

But his question rang in my ears. What *did* I want to do? I hadn't the foggiest idea, so I changed the subject. "Is your brother always like that?" I asked.

"Claude?"

"No."

"Marcel?"

I shook my head. "Eric."

"Ah! The ugly one," Beau said. "No, he's not always like that. Sometimes he's worse."

I waited for Beau to continue but he didn't. So I said, "How can you stand it?"

He shrugged. "My dad says my uncle Jorge was always pounding on him as a kid. It's a brother thing."

"But you're nice to your other brothers."

"*I*," Beau said, poking himself in the chest, "am an infinitely superior human being to both my brother Eric and my uncle Jorge."

"Infinitely," I agreed. "Are your dad and your uncle friends now?" I asked.

Beau laughed. "We only hear from Uncle Jorge when he needs money."

When I went upstairs, Dad had the TV back on. "All is forgiven," he said, nodding toward the phone. "The womenfolk are bringing lunch tomorrow."

I didn't know what to think about that. Was there any truth to the swimsuit story? I shrugged to myself. Another mystery. One among many. Like: Would Cora still be around next summer, Muzak, gum chewing, and all? What if Dad married her? Would they keep her cats? Where would that leave me? In a hotel?

I looked at Dad, propped up on his pillows, and told myself I'd worry about all that later. Or, as Jet says, "I'll jump off that bridge when I get to it."

We had pizza delivered and ate it on Dad's bed. There was an old movie on and I didn't mind watching it. The bad guy reminded me of Eric, so when the movie was over, I told Dad about Eric always beating up on Beau.

Dad rubbed his stubbly chin. "Sorry to hear that," he said. "I never noticed." How could he not have noticed? I wondered briefly. But I suppose that just because Beau was paying close attention to my dad, it didn't necessarily mean Dad was paying attention back. Then, without even meaning to, I told him about Alex.

"Edgar White," Dad replied. "I guess everyone's got one."

"Huh?"

"A bully. Mine was Edgar White. I'll never forget that name. I spent years hoping I'd run into him again so I could punch his lights out."

I waited for him to go on.

"I vowed I'd never be picked on again. Started lifting weights and slugging away at the punching bag, pretending it was his face." Dad smiled. "Edgar White's what made me start working out, so I guess something good came of it. Until then I was this skinny." He held up his finger. "Edgar White was big and beefy. Mean as sin. Had three goons who did whatever he said." Dad shook his head. "They got me on the way home from school once. Four against one."

"What did you do?" I asked.

"Fought for my life."

"Alex never actually touched me," I said. "Just took my books, called me Worm. But it was for a whole school year."

Dad shook his head again. "Hard being a kid," he said. "I forget that." He took the last, cold piece of pizza and chewed awhile. Then he said, "I thought bullies were a thing of the past, that kids were smarter now, more civilized and sophisticated than in my day. I see how much more articulate and thoughtful you are than I was as a boy, and I hoped life was different for your generation. Better."

"I wish," I said.

Dad nodded. "Well, maybe it'll be better for *your* son," he said. "Or your grandson."

My son? The idea made me laugh. But then I imagined myself as an old guy with a busted knee and my nerdy kid telling me he's getting picked on by bullies. I guess I'd tell him about Alex. Maybe mention Edgar White too.

"Dad," I said, "can I ask you something?"

"Fire away."

"Remember that guy Chris who called? When I forgot to give you his message?"

Dad nodded.

"How come he didn't know you had a son?"

Dad shrugged and looked like he was going to joke about it, but then he stopped himself and said, "I'm sorry, John. Everyone'll know I have a son from now on."

chapter fourteen

The next day Cora and Iris brought fried chicken, potato salad, garlic rolls, watermelon, and cherry pie. I ate like a pig. I was in no shape for swimming, but Iris insisted. She practically dragged me out the door, whispering that we should leave the two lovebirds alone.

When we got outside, she said, "Thanks for breaking your father's leg."

"No problem," I said.

We knocked on Beau's door. Then the three of us headed down to the pool. I could tell Beau had an instant crush on Iris by the way he walked slumped over. Plus, he did some fancy dives I'd never seen him do before.

It's harder to tell with girls, but I thought Iris might like him too, because when we played Marco Polo, she always followed Beau's voice. I didn't mind *too* much. I was leaving anyway. Maybe Cora would start bringing Iris over, and she and Beau could hang out together, go to the diner, eat salt.

I was glad that Eric didn't show up to pick on Beau in front of Iris. But after a while, Beau's mom came out on the balcony and called down, "Beau, Sweetie! Will you take the boys for a minute? I need a shower!"

Beau didn't grumble—not even about being called Sweetie in front of a girl. I *hated* it when my mom called me Honey or Cutie in front of *anyone*.

Beau hauled himself out of the pool and ran dripping up the stairs. Then he came back down with Marcel wiggling in his arms and Claude skipping along next to him.

Iris said Beau's brothers were adorable and she thought Beau was a terrific big brother. I could tell she liked that in a person. I guess Beau was right about the chick-magnet thing.

When we were leaving the pool, Beau pulled me aside. I figured he was going to tell me he liked Iris, but he said, "I told His Ugliness about you and Chet Carter."

"Yeah?"

"He practically peed his pants!" Beau said, laughing. Cackling, actually, all the way back to his apartment. Claude and even baby Marcel joined in the laughter. The three of them sounded slightly insane.

Iris looked puzzled.

"It's a long story," I told her.

Back inside Dad's apartment, Cora had her camera out and was taking pictures of Dad in his cast.

"Take one of me and John!" Iris said, grabbing my arm. We were both still in our bathing suits and shivery from the pool. I could feel the goose bumps on Iris's arm.

Cora took two pictures. "I'll send you prints," she said, and I almost liked her. I pictured Brad and Theo green with envy.

While Iris and I had been down at the pool, Cora had helped Dad take a shower without getting his cast wet. And she'd held the mirror so he could shave sitting down. I never would've thought of that. Dad seemed as happy as a clam and Cora was practically purring.

When they said good-bye to each other, Iris whispered to me, "Well, see ya at the wedding, maybe."

"Yours and Beau's?"

Iris shoved me and shrieked, "Shut up!" She must've liked Beau even more than I'd thought. Then she said, "No, Scarecrow, I meant my aunt and your dad's wedding! Then we'll be kin. I'll call you Cousin Kansas. How's that?"

"Beats being called Scarecrow and Tin Man," I said.

"Sorry, Lion." Iris giggled, darting out the door. At least she hadn't called me Dorothy.

Beau's question from the night before had been brewing in my brain long enough. What did *I* want to do? By the time Iris and Cora left, I knew the answer. So, I just up and asked Dad if he'd like me to come back over my winter break. I didn't get all fidgety and hangdog about it. I didn't beg or anything. I just *asked.* It wasn't hard.

"You'd do that?" Dad asked, surprised. "You'd come twice a year?"

"Of course I would," I answered. "Sure."

"That would be *terrific!*" Dad said. "Absolutely terrific!" And I could tell he meant it. We grinned and grinned at each other like two goofs.

"No Rollerblading, though," I finally said.

Dad laughed. "You're right. We better stick to hang gliding and bungee jumping."

I called home to tell my mom to expect me the next day as planned. Jet answered the phone.

"Jet!" I said. "You're back!"

"Your sister sent up smoke signals summoning me," he joked. I guess he meant her bonfire on the stove.

"I did not!" Liz squealed in the background. Then she must've grabbed the phone. "John?" she said.

"Yep."

"Jet was camped out in his car in front of the house for so long, I finally took pity on the neighbors, who, needless to say, were getting a little freaked. I let him back on *probation.*"

"Glad to hear it," I said. Then I told her I'd be home the next day.

"Good," Liz said. "Mom's been in a state, and I couldn't bear another week of worry patrol on my own! How's the Phantom's knee?"

"The knee's bad, but the Phantom is great," I said. "He thinks you're *classy,* by the way. And remind me to tell you what he said about your Barbie and Ken dolls."

"Huh?"

"Liz," I said, "why don't cannibals eat clowns?"

"Why?" she asked with a giggle ready in her voice. Liz loves jokes, the dumber the better. When I told her the punch line, she burst out laughing. I knew she'd tell it to Jet the second she got off the phone.

I hung up, smiling.

The next morning I helped Dad hop out to the living room. Then I made him some eggs. There was no trace of the mess Beau and I had made in the kitchen. Cora must've cleaned it the day before. I almost felt guilty, but then I figured she owed it to me—she'd never paid back my two dollars.

When Dad reached for the TV remote, I snatched it away from him. "Hey!" he said.

Beau appeared at the door with a plate of muffins from his mom.

"My cab'll be here in forty-five minutes," I said, hinting that Beau should split.

He got it and did an immediate about-face. "I'll be back in forty-three," he said.

"Wait!" I said. "Hey, Dad, how 'bout giving Beau a key, just in case?" I turned to Beau. "That'll be your what, seventh, besides your own?"

Dad agreed, so I gave Beau mine. If anyone had told me a week ago that I'd be giving Beau the key to my dad's apartment—or for that matter that I'd be the one to tell Dad to make up with *Cora*—well, I *really* would've thought they were nuts. Weird week in Dadland, that's for sure.

"I'll need that key back in December," I said. "When I come."

"Cool!" Beau said, and banged out the door.

Soon it was time. Dad was stuck in his chair, so the good-bye was up to me. I decided, What the heck, and went over. I handed Dad back his remote, then knelt down and gave him a hug. Dad thumped me on the back a couple of times, then grabbed me and hugged me back for real.

Beau walked me downstairs to wait for my cab. "I'll keep an eye on two sixteen," he said.

"Thanks," I said. "Call or e-mail if anything comes up, okay?" I gave him my info. I'd written Iris's phone number down too, and when Beau's eyes got to it, I saw him start to blush.

Then Eric appeared around the corner and came straight for us. What new abuse would he trot out this time? I wondered. But he did something I never would've predicted: He smiled at me. And, as if that weren't weird enough, he said, "Hey, man, is it true you know Chet Carter?"

"Yeah," I answered.

My taxi pulled up.

"So what's he like? Like, what kinda guy is he?" Eric asked.

"He's really nice," I said.

The driver opened the trunk and I put my suitcase in.

"I was wondering," Eric said, looking almost nervous, "if you'd, like, give him a tape of mine to, like, listen to or something. Let me know what he thinks, maybe."

I looked from Eric to Beau, then back at Eric. "Sure," I said. "Why don't you have Beau mail it to me sometime and I'll do that?"

"I could run upstairs and grab a tape right now," Eric said.

I pointed to the cab. "Sorry. I gotta go."

"It'll just take a second," Eric whined.

I opened the car door and got in, saying, "Just get my address from Beau."

Then I saluted Beau, whose smile was even bigger and goofier than usual, and shut the door behind me. As we pulled away from the curb, I thought, Yesss! Now Eric has *got* to be nice to Beau. I hoped Beau would hold out for a l-o-n-g time. Years! Make Eric grovel, beg for my address. Ha! Wait till I tell Theo!

First I was just grinning, but then I started laughing. And then I couldn't stop. It turned into a full-blown screaming meemie attack right there in the cab. But the driver didn't bat an eye. Maybe people got hysterical alone in L.A. taxis all the time.

After I'd calmed down some, I gradually realized that Ditz wasn't going to greet me when I got home, and now I was going to have to face that. I told myself that maybe I'd blotch like Beau. Maybe I'd sob the way Iris said Cora did. Maybe I'd be stone-faced like Dad. But one way or another, I'd be okay—more or less, eventually, probably.

I'd never taken a cab alone before. Never gotten myself to the airport, checked my suitcase, or found my gate all by myself. But it went off without a hitch.

As soon as I sat down, a flight attendant crouched next to

me and said, "If you need anything, young man, you just let me know. Okay?"

I almost told her I wasn't as young as I looked—almost said, "My dad was short too, till high school." But I heard Beau's voice in my head saying, "Harsh! Harsh words on an airplane!"

So I smiled at the attendant. "Thanks," I said. "I'm sure I'll be fine. Just fine."